1. **This book may be kept three weeks. It is to be returned on / before the last date stamped below.**
2. **A fine of 25c will be charged for every week or part of week a book is overdue.**

A note on the Author

Israeli-born Ronit Lentin came to Ireland in 1969, where she worked in television and as a freelance journalist. She published several novellas in Hebrew and a book of dialogues with Palestinian women activists (Jerusalem, 1982). Her novella *Tea with Mrs Klein* was published in 1985 by Wolfhound Press, and her novel *Night Train to Mother* was published in 1989 by Attic Press and by Cleis Press in the USA in 1990. She teaches sociology and women's studies at Trinity College, Dublin. She is married to television producer Louis Lentin and they have two adult children.

Songs on the
Death of Children

RONIT LENTIN

POOLBEG

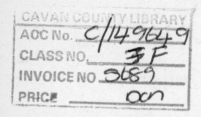
Published in 1996
by Poolbeg Press Ltd
123 Baldoyle Industrial Estate
Dublin 13, Ireland

© Ronit Lentin 1996

The moral right of the author has been asserted.

The Publishers gratefully acknowledge the support of The Arts Council.

A catalogue record for this book is available from the British Library.

ISBN 1 85371 625 1

Cover painting by Yosl Bergner
Cover design by Poolbeg Group Services Ltd
Set by Poolbeg Group Services Ltd in Times 10.5/14
Printed by The Guernsey Press Ltd,
Vale, Guernsey, Channel Islands.

To Alana and Miki, with my love

I would never have allowed the children to go out;
They carried them away,
And I could not protest.
In this weather, in this wind
I would never have allowed the children to go out
For fear they might become ill.
But these are idle thoughts.
In this weather, in this horror
I would never have allowed the children to go out,
I feared they might die tomorrow.
I do not have this fear any more.
In this weather, in this wind, in this storm
They rest as if they were in their mother's house.
Not scared by any tempest.
Protected by God's hand.

"In this weather, in this storm." The last song in Gustav
Mahler's song cycle *Kindertotenlieder*, based on poems
by Friedrich Rueckert.

PART ONE

CHAPTER ONE

"Did anyone give you anything to take with you?" a young, very tanned, black-haired woman asked, looking at my passport at the EL AL check-in desk in Heathrow.

"What do you mean?" I was impatient. Kept waiting almost half an hour in a slow queue.

"I mean, did you pack your cases yourself and are you bringing anything which someone else gave you?"

"Yes, I packed myself and no, I am not bringing anything like that." I expected security, but this was a bit much.

"What is the purpose of your visit to Israel?" Nothing if not persistent.

"Aren't we getting a bit nosy?" I said. "I am a visitor. That should be enough."

"We would like to ascertain the purpose of your visit," the young woman insisted. I saw her beckon a young, surprisingly blond, man to join her. "I am a journalist and I am going to cover Israel for my newspaper."

The young woman and her blond companion exchanged glances. Asked about my paper. Its circulation. Its political orientation. My precise job. How many years I had been there. They were not familiar with Irish newspapers, they explained politely but firmly, avoiding my eyes. I replied as best as I could without losing my frayed temper. What are

3

they on about? I am a Jew, I wanted to shout, just like you, but I wouldn't give them the satisfaction.

"You must excuse our questions," the young man said finally, this time looking me straight in the eye. "As a journalist, you must remember that unfortunate young Irishwoman who was made to carry a bomb on to an EL AL plane. We want to make absolutely sure." I couldn't help wondering about those blue eyes.

"Yes, of course." Damn, I thought as they rummaged through my neatly-packed case, unfolding every pair of carefully-folded knickers, unscrewing mascaras, disturbing tidily-rolled tights. Just like the North. Soon they'll want to strip search me.

"This is terrific," I said between clenched teeth as they handed me the case to close. What a mess."

"Sorry, Miss Goldman," the woman said coolly. "You are going to a war zone, you know. Which is probably why you are going there in the first place, no?"

"Too right. Have you quite finished with me?"

"Quite? What do you mean? We have completely finished with you," the young man said, oblivious to the subtleties of the language. "Thank you and have a nice stay in Israel." Smiling into my eyes again.

"Please take your case with you to the boarding area," the woman said. "You'll be asked to identify it before boarding."

I lifted my case on to a trolley. Just as well I didn't tell them what I was really going to do.

"A book about women?" colleagues asked when I told them of my idea. "Are you moving to the lifestyle section?"

I was known as a hardline investigative political reporter. A coverer of trouble spots. Hated the idea of women's pages and women's issues and used to say that it was time, now

4

that the women's movement had gained momentum even in staid Ireland, that women started to read the whole paper, from sports to finance. There was no need, I argued, much to the annoyance of feminist colleagues, to make things easier for women. And anyway, if a social issue is important enough, there was no reason why men should not read it too.

It was Alison who changed my mind. Alison. Beautiful, sad Alison. Abused sexually and physically by her alcoholic father and finally made pregnant by him. I met her when child abuse became a prime news topic and Don sent me to find an abuse victim, present time. "None of your middle-aged ladies who think they remember having been abused twenty years ago. I want the real thing, pain and gut feelings." I hated when he spoke like a tabloid editor, which was more and more often these days.

Alison. Sad Alison. Lanky hair falling on half-closed eyes. Fingers tremblingly holding an extinguished cigarette. Beautiful face. But pale, tired. She arrived at our meeting-place in a short-skirted convent uniform. Alison. It took me three hours to make her talk. There were many long silences. Intelligent. Eaten by fears. Alison insisted she wanted to see my copy before it went to press. Looking into these sad, beaten eyes, I agreed, much to Don's anger. "You know we never allow it," he shouted across his desk.

"Tough. I've already promised. Without it there's no story."

"Is it worth it?"

"Fuck off, Don." I turned to walk away from his office.

"I asked if it's worth it," Don said slowly. "Because if it isn't, there's no point in arguing over her seeing the copy."

"It's worth it. It'll turn the stomachs of your Sunday morning readers."

"Good," Don said. "That's what I like to hear. Let her see the damn copy."

"You're so generous." I turned to go.

"Am I seeing you tonight?" Don asked my moving back.

I stopped. "The price a woman has to pay in this establishment to get what she wants," I said affecting a sigh.

Alison. I shuddered as I sat in the crowded departure lounge. The poor mite. It was Alison who was responsible for my sitting here. But would these security bastards understand if I tried to explain? I had made the changes she asked for without putting up a fight.

"Imagine me trying to alter your precious copy." Don laughed, nervous. "There would be war over every semicolon."

"You should know by now that I don't use semicolons," I retorted, only half angry.

That night we made love tentatively, with my mind on Alison and her father. I could see him thrusting into her, his fists beating her face as he was coming. I could see him weeping drunkenly at the foot of her bed when she told him she was pregnant. I could see his unshaven face staring at her tearfully when she told him she was leaving his house. I could see Alison running down the street and her father after her with a kitchen knife. And I could see her mother beaten after she helped her daughter leave home.

When at ten-thirty Don got up, gulped the remains of the rancid wine and said he had to go home, I thought, go home. Go home to your lovely wife and daughters. I didn't see him to the door as usual and returned to the crumpled bed to change the bed-linen, suddenly repelled by the thought of sleeping on the soiled sheets.

Alison. The article aroused the strongest reaction. More

than anything I had ever written. I was invited to appear on television and spoke about the plight of Ireland's hidden abuse victims. It was time, I said, looking directly at camera one although I was supposed to look at the interviewer, that we broke the conspiracy of silence – the title of the article.

Alison rang after the television programme and asked to see me again. We met in a coffee shop above *Next* in Grafton Street where I had just begun to buy my businesslike clothes. Me in my trendy trouser suit and Alison in her school uniform, her stomach well rounded now and her face paler.

She was living with a foster-family until the baby came. Her father had been arrested and was to face trial. Alison didn't look as frightened as before but her eyes were larger and bluer.

"You were good on television," she started. I shrugged. We talked on for a while. Alison spoke of her new life, and how her mother was coming to terms with bringing her husband to court.

"It's hard on her too," Alison said. "But I can't help feeling angry at her for letting him do it to me. I'm learning to be angry. In therapy."

I realised I too had been angry since I met Alison. Angry at parents, at men, at a society which allowed a young, bright girl to be molested and did nothing. My anger was crystal clear but something deeper was bothering me. Keeping me awake at night. Father came to mind. Father and his secrets. But I could put no words to this new sensation.

I don't remember at what stage the conversation turned. Suddenly Alison was angry at me too. She didn't say anything, but the sense of outrage, of having been used for a good story, came through. As did her fear of the future. I came out of the meeting confused. When I told Don of the meeting, all he could think of asking was if there was a follow-up story there.

I had met Don when I came for my first interview with the editor three years ago. It was a wet day and my hair was soaking. I can still see Don's look when he passed me in the corridor outside the editor's office. Later he confessed he had fallen for me that moment. A drenched little ugly duckling. Fresh from the suburbs, eager to impress the editor with my honours degree and the experience I clocked up working for the local community magazine.

"You were simply magnificent, like a small-town American kid who becomes a big star which, of course, you are now," he often told me since.

I was taken on as part of the policy of recruiting young reporters in an attempt to attract a young readership. As news editor, Don was an exacting taskmaster. Always after blood and guts. Let them have it, Patsy. Let them choke on their croissants and coffee, those Dublin four hypocrites.

He started taking me with him to receptions and to liquid lunches. I accepted his invitations, flattered. Liquid lunches soon went on to become late-night bites after the Saturday night shifts. I used to love the frenzied Saturday night panics, the squabbling over headlines and front-page stories, ending each Saturday night session high on adrenalin.

I had never had a boyfriend. Father frowned upon boyfriends. No one was good enough for his Patricia. Sex had never been mentioned at home. An austere home, lacking in sensuality. At twenty-three I was still, unbelievably, a virgin. Sex, real sex, was frightening, confusing, even sordid.

One Saturday night, after dinner at the *Trocadero*, Don drove me home. Outside the flat he put his hand between my thighs, tightly clad in a pair of jeans. I felt a new, shivering sensation and when he followed this with a kiss, his tongue searching my mouth demandingly, I found myself responding with my whole body. Don, who had been drinking red wine for two hours previously, asked if he could come up. My body prompted me and all the way up to the third floor, he touched me with an urgency I had never known before.

We fell on to the unmade bed. Don unzipped his trousers and at the same time undid mine and the sex was fast, hot, coming to an abrupt end.

Numb, I felt only a dull ache. Don rolled off and, to my amazement, began to cry softly. "I'm sorry, Pat. I'm sorry. I wanted to do this. So much. Ever since I first met you. I didn't know. I'm sorry." His words in fits and starts, between sobs. I stroked his head without knowing what I was doing as he lay, half-dressed, sobbing between the sheet and the duvet. He cried for a long time, until he cried himself to sleep. He woke half an hour later, sat up suddenly, looked at the green digits of the bedside clock-radio and whispered, "Oh, my God. It's almost three." He started to get up but changed his mind and turned to me. Unable to sleep, I had been watching him.

"I'm sorry about earlier. I had no idea. I didn't know I was the first," he muttered, his embarrassment untypical. "I haven't cried like that since I was a kid." He looked at me almost tenderly. "You're so beautiful, damn it," he spat. "I don't want to let you go. Ever." He touched my hair with the back of his hand. The gentlest gesture I had ever seen him make. "Must go now," he whispered. "You know I'm married," he added, a question-mark in his now soft voice. I had heard, but had never before bothered to think about it.

9

Until then I had been simply going out with my news editor to receptions where I was introduced as the new young reporter, whose articles were beginning to be noticed. The odd late-night meal didn't mean much either. We had been working late and I shrugged off his attentions as harmless flirtations. If I had suspected he was serious about me, I never acknowledged it. But now I felt suddenly trapped. And the cloying intimacy of his crying was frightening.

"Why don't you just go home and forget about the whole thing?"

"I couldn't forget about it," he said. "You've touched me. Will you let me see you again? Please?"

When he left, I lay awake for hours. I had kept myself apart, almost aloof. When pursued, I found ways of rejecting suitors, a habit I acquired while still in Father's house, when I knew I couldn't risk bringing anyone home, to our tight circle, which felt crystal hard. Intimacy had always frightened me. Now, I knew, my circle had been interrupted, my aloneness challenged.

My first big investigative piece was to appear the following morning and the prospect of seeing my byline on the front page, coupled with Don's invasion of my life, was strangely exciting.

I can't remember falling in love with Don. But he pursued me insistently, on and off the newsroom floor. And I allowed myself to be taken over. I had never taken any initiative in relationships, with men or with women, reserving all my energies for work. I was aware people were saying I was sleeping my way to the top. When I got one of the top journalistic awards only eighteen months after joining the paper, I felt vindicated. Yet I never felt quite clean.

I tried to explain my involvement with Don to my school-

10

friend Marianne, stressing the difference with what I saw as her dead-end affair with John Kelly, an estate agent for whom she was working.

"Why do you think your affair is any different?" Marianne said acidly, the first time I told her.

"It's obvious," I said without thinking. "Don is a much more liberal man. He doesn't run home for his tea at six o'clock and we don't screw on the office desk."

Marianne said nothing for a while. Later, when we were talking about something completely different, she said softly, "Wait. Your affair will turn sour too. At least I know mine is a no-hoper."

I tried to reason with her, explained that Don was a conscientious man. That affairs didn't happen often in his life. That he had said again and again how much I mattered. How much he loved me. But I wasn't even convincing myself.

Marianne listened quietly and then said, "But he isn't leaving his wife, is he?"

I laughed. "Why should he leave his wife, for God's sake? For one thing, I don't want to marry him. What would a nice Jewish girl like me do with an ex-priest? There are not only two children, but also the dregs of religious guilt to cope with. I've enough of him the way we are. I would never want to marry him."

Marianne smiled. "There must be something about nice Jewish girls like us that we don't mind being their little bits on the side. There must be some pay-off." And she got up and left the room.

That was almost three years ago, I thought, my lower back aching from sitting on the airport seat. Three years ago I was as naive as Marianne had been when she first started sleeping with that jerk Kelly. She knew more than I did then. She knew all about men who wanted to have their cake and eat it. I had chosen to have this affair.

With time, Don wanted more and more of me, leaving no time for other people. I became a virtual recluse, waited for him on my free evenings, kept the phone free for his frequent calls. He phoned several times each day and night, starting early in the morning, right after he took his daughters to school. Speaking from his study, where his wife could not hear, his words caressing my body, awakening my desire. After these early calls, I could no longer sleep.

He would catch me again before I left home to be in for eleven. From behind the closed door of his office, where he was going through the post and reading the morning papers. Throughout the day we would discuss news, politics, world events: our conversations helping me, I knew, to become a top commentator, envied by most and cherished by the paper.

When I went away on a job, his phone calls pursued me through the day, solicitous, erotic. Usually his last call was in the early hours of the morning, long after his wife had fallen asleep. He filled my days with his enquiries, interrogated me about every moment spent without him.

And he was hellishly jealous. Every man I spoke to was a suitable target. Did you fancy him? What did he say? Did he ask you out? Did he touch you? The odd evening I spent with friends, he would find me and phone me there, or phone the friends after I left. Keeping tabs, reminding me of Father. Was Don a replacement for Father? Leaving the daughter no choice?

My days were full of his probing pursuits, I told Marianne when I was home in the suburbs. Don would chase me with endless calls and Mother was becoming impatient.

"Who is this man? Why don't you bring him home?" So I made my visits less frequent. But I missed Marianne, the only friend I could confide in outside the world of journalism. I had never been able to talk to Mother and Marianne and I shared our secrets, adding another confidence to the family secrets. Every so often Marianne asked, "why do you let him monopolise you like this? Why don't you simply leave?"

I would shrug. I thought we loved each other, although I never used that word. Love. It felt all wrong. I allowed him to fill my world. Left no room for anything else. And, of course, I was indebted to him for the contacts I made, the stories I was covering.

Don was my first lover, leading me slowly through the labyrinth of sexual pleasure. It was an adult, erotic relationship, marred only by his obsession about spending the end of each night in his marital bed. From time to time he managed to arrange journeys when we could spend whole nights or even weekends together. And I was so grateful, I never considered the humiliation. What I didn't confide, even to Marianne, was how Don allowed me to remain a child, passive in my dependence, captive of my secrets, a familiar valley where death and defeat reigned undisturbed. He was in my blood, I told Marianne, who smiled and said, "I know what you mean. I wish I could get that bastard Kelly out of mine."

But I still thought there was a difference.

Then Marianne became pregnant. Kelly refused to use anything because of his religion and she forgot her pill one night. I accompanied her to London and stayed with her for the abortion. Marianne did not return to Kelly and to the suburb. Liberated by her rage, she stayed in London to work as an executive secretary. "If only I'd known how much more money I could have made, I would have left ages ago," she said.

After the abortion trip I could no longer refuse to acknowledge the parallels. Kelly, who wouldn't use contraception, yet had an affair with a young unmarried woman who worked for him for years, was just another Don, who swore he could not live without me. I began to understand that if it came to the crunch, he would stick by his wife and let me take the boat.

Don thought I was mad when, on my return from the abortion trip, I broke down, accusing him of hypocrisy and deceit.

"I don't want to be with someone who has not only left his vocation, but who is cheating the woman who had given up so much to marry him, a fallen priest. I don't want someone who keeps chasing me, without a moment's peace, yet is never able to spend a whole night with me," I screamed. "You are a deceiver, a user. How can I ever trust you?"

Don held me. Things would change, he promised. Not that he promised to leave his wife. He couldn't. Not after what she had been through. But we would spend more time together. And he would stop pestering. Stop his phone calls. I was young and needed the company of young people. He wanted me to have fun, enjoy myself, he said as I cried silently in his arms. We made love and I lay immobile and numb as he crept out of my bed at midnight. To go home.

Things did not change much. My addiction to secrets kept me chained. I wrote a series of articles about abortion and the letter pages were full of reactions for and against. Don

14

continued to phone several times each day. I was too busy to keep him at bay. I was asked on to a women's radio programme to discuss the realities of abortion on post-abortion-referendum Ireland. The paper began to use my photograph and the series got me the *Woman Journalist of the Year* award. But I still allowed Don to creep out of my bed before midnight.

Despite the success of the abortion series, I still shunned women's issues. "I won't be labelled," I said again and again as women's organisations asked me to speak, open seminars, address symposia. "Women's issues are only good enough if they make a strong news story. Otherwise, forget it."

But then came Alison. After my second meeting with her, I told Don I wouldn't see him again. I remembered it vividly now as the flight was being announced. Don came over after work as usual. He had a bottle of Muscadet which he asked me to put in the fridge so we could have a sip later. I took the bottle from his hand and threw it on the kitchen floor. As the bottle shattered, Don grabbed me but my body was rigid. "What's the matter with you, Patsy?" he said plaintively. He pulled me hard to his body. I could feel his erection against my crotch and tried to remain unmoved.

"I am never sleeping with you again." I released myself from his grip and stood firmly in front of him.

"Why?"

"Because I've had it. I've had this humiliation you call love."

"Humiliation?"

"Look, Don," I tried to sound reasonable even though I was burning to break a few more things. "This isn't going anywhere. You're no better than Alison's bastard of a father. A user."

15

"Ah," his voice assumed the usual cynicism he employed in most of his dealings at work. "So it has to do with that little bitch. You saw her again today, didn't you?"

"Don't call her a little bitch," I screamed. "She's suffered enough without fascist news editors calling her a bitch."

"Anyway, what's the connection between her creep of a father and me? You were a consenting adult, remember." His voice remained harsh.

"Some adult," I said. "I don't want you near me any more. Get out of my house."

"Don't be silly, Patsy," he said. He was the only person I let call me Patsy. Mother called me Patricia, as did my school-friends, but I preferred Pat. "I can't leave like that. Let's talk."

I started to clear the floor, not taking care to avoid the glass shards.

"Careful. Let me do it," Don said. "You mustn't get glass into your hands." He grabbed the floorcloth. "Don't you have a mop?"

I sat on the kitchen chair, suddenly exhausted. "Leave it. It's too late for grand gestures."

Don left the floorcloth and turned me to face him, holding my face in his hands, moving me towards his body. He caressed my face, drawing it close to him, but I shook my head free and stood up to face him. "If you must, let's talk," I said. "But without your usual cynicism. There was no need to call Alison a bitch. She's damn all to do with it." I was losing the argument, allowing him to take the lead. As always.

"Rubbish," Don said. "You lost your head when you did her story. You got too emotionally involved. A dangerous thing for an investigative journalist like you. There's nothing

16

wrong with you and me. You've always said you didn't want to marry me."

"Marrying you has nothing to do with what's wrong with us. You simply took me over. I was young then but I'm no longer young."

We talked for hours that night, I remembered, as I moved in line into the baggage area where I identified my cases. And I knew I would stay with him. Knew it was I who was allowing him to lure me further into his net. Knew it was my choice to remain led, to stay in the honeyed trap of the secrets. And we did end up having sex that night. Heaped passively on my bed, I allowed Don to make love to me. All the while seeing Alison's father thrusting into his sad daughter and slapping her bruised face.

I entered the plane where, in front of me, a group of men in black caftans and thin beards talked nervously in a language I identified as Yiddish. A distant memory.

When I found my seat, I closed my eyes and thought of Alison's end. I had heard of Alison's death on *Morning Ireland* after Don's morning call. "A fifteen-year-old pregnant schoolgirl was found dead in the bedroom she shared with another girl at a foster home in Dublin earlier this morning," the newsreader read. "The gardai do not suspect foul play."

I knew immediately the dead girl was Alison. Numb, I dressed mechanically, preparing to go out and get the story when Don's second call that morning reached me. "It's your girl, Patsy. You heard, yes?" Without awaiting my reply, he added curtly, "See that you get the whole story, Patsy," his voice businesslike. He must have been speaking from the kitchen, where his wife was serving the porridge. I drove all the way to Alison's northside foster-home, paying no

17

attention to red lights or other cars. I hurried into the house. Alison's foster-mother, a plump social worker in a stained navy jogging suit and slippers, was comforting an older woman. They had been crying and when Jeanne saw me, her face stretched in a tired smile.

"Pat, how good of you to come," she said, her voice tearful and hoarse. "This is Patricia Goldman," she said to the other woman. "The one who wrote about Alison, remember?" The older woman looked me in the face, her gaze impassive. "This is Alison's mother, Mary," Jeanne said. I returned the stare. I saw a face, not unlike Alison's. With much pain engraved in the tiny wrinkles around the dark blue eyes.

"I rushed over the minute I heard," I said. "What happened? She seemed to be doing so well."

"Doing well, not doing well, what does it all matter now?" Alison's mother said hoarsely. "She's dead. My Alison's dead." She started sobbing and, as Jeanne put her arm around her, she collapsed on to the floor where she was standing.

I helped Jeanne get her up and lay her on the sofa. "Tell me, what really happened?"

"It's a long story. Come back later and we'll talk. Must look after Mary now. The poor woman. She feels so guilty. There's no point saying anything to her right now. Feels she could have stopped it if she really tried. But the bastard abused her too. Used to beat her up most days and, if she dared breathe a word about the way he treated Alison, he would tie her to the bed and make her watch. And things aren't much better now that he's awaiting trial. Women like her never get treatment because they don't think themselves worthy of therapy. Too much guilt. Sure, *I* feel guilty too. If only I could have stopped her." Jeanne stopped, handed me a cup of instant coffee and shrugged. "Are you here for a story, or on a courtesy call?"

"I came as soon as I heard. But before I had a chance to leave the house, my news editor rang. He wants the full story for Sunday."

Jeanne's face fell. "So you're after the story. Like the rest."

"Don't do that to me, Jeanne. I'm broken by the news. She was doing so well. Journalists too have a heart. But we have a job to do. And you're better off with me writing it than if some hack snoops around."

"I suppose so. But I'd prefer it if you came later," Jeanne said.

"OK," I said. "But can I see her? Please?"

Jeanne said nothing. She led me upstairs to where Alison's body lay covered in a pale peach sheet, her long legs sticking out. I lifted the sheet carefully to reveal Alison's pale face. Poor Alison. Poor, poor Alison.

"They're coming to take her away to the coroner's soon," Jeanne said.

I made straight for Don's office. I went in without knocking, ignoring Roisín, his secretary, who said loudly, "He has people with him, Pat. Shall I let him know you're here?"

"Don't bother," I said, walking into Don's office. He was looking at photographs with two staff photographers.

"Can I have a word?" I said loudly, making the three men look up.

Don took one look at me and said to the men, "Give me a moment." He escorted them to the door which he closed behind him. "What's the story?"

"No story, yet. I'm to go back to the house in an hour or

19

so. Her mother was there but she was too upset, so I said I'd come back later."

"Damn it, Patsy. You should have stayed. Did you get to see the body?"

"Yes, I saw it. I'm going back, Don, but not to do the story. Send Seán. Or Orla. I'm not doing it."

"What's the matter, Patsy?" All the time looking me straight in the eye.

"The matter is that a girl I cared for killed herself early this morning because it hurt too much. And I'm not going to use her death to get another scoop. We've done well enough out of her, don't you think?"

"You're upset," Don said, his voice softening. "Why don't you have a drink? You'll feel better."

"Fuck off, Don. I'll never feel better about that kid's death. It's my fault, too, can't you see? I don't want a drink. What I need is a good weep with Alison's mother and foster-mother. I wish I could cry, damn it. I'm taking two days leave. I'm due leave."

I turned to leave. But Don grabbed my arm. "Where do you think you're going? I haven't said you can take time off. We're short-staffed and Alison's death is the most important story of the week. And it's you who knows the story inside out. How would we look on Sunday with a Mickey Mouse story by Seán or Orla?"

"Frankly, I don't give a shit." I released my arm, using all the force I could muster. "And now, if you'll excuse me." I left his office without turning back and went straight into the car, where I sat for a long time in the middle of the crowded car park staring blankly ahead.

Was I waiting for Don to come and talk sense to me, I wondered as I settled into my seat, putting on the safety belt,

20

listening to the safety instructions in Hebrew, English and French. Don didn't follow me into the car park and I drove back to Jeanne's house, stopping on the way to buy a bar of Cadbury's *Wholenut*, which I always consumed ravenously when upset. The door was open and as I entered, Alison's body was carted into an ambulance. Inside, in the darkened living-room, her mother lay sobbing with Jeanne sitting beside her, caressing her face with her broad hand.

Jeanne turned towards me but said nothing. She motioned me not to disturb Mary. "I want you to know I'm not doing the story," I whispered. "I told them I didn't want to get another ride on poor Alison. My news editor is fuming, but I told him to get lost."

Jeanne smiled, her face sagging. "Go into the kitchen. Tony will get you a cup of tea and I'll be with you soon."

Mary lifted her head. "Is this reporter girl here again, Jeanne?" she asked, her voice small. "Don't worry, love, she's not reporting. She's back because she cared about your Alison," Jeanne hugged Mary's fat body. "There, there, you're doing fine, love." Mary continued sobbing softly. Her big body heaving. Her sobs like retching, long, pained.

I went up to Alison's room. The empty bed had been tidied. On the desk her school books and copybooks lay neatly. At the edge of the bed a small battered teddy bear, his glass eyes staring at the still room. I stood there for what seemed like hours, looking at the tidy remains of Alison's spent childhood. This was where Jeanne found me. "There's a call for you. From your office."

"Do you mind telling them I've left?"

"As you wish." Jeanne turned to go.

I stayed in Alison's room alone. It was my second encounter with death. Father's had been the first. But death, I

21

was beginning to realise, was an omnipresence, with Father and Mother's untold past hovering in Alison's empty bedroom like a bird of prey.

It was late afternoon before I heard the whole story. Alison's father had managed to smuggle a letter which was delivered to her at school by a released prisoner. The letter, which Jeanne found under Alison's pillow early that morning when her roommate's screams woke up the house, was a love letter from a desperate man to the woman of his dreams. It was not only erotic, full of sexual connotations, which, Jeanne said, she was sure Alison had been too naive to take in, it was also full of menace. He would take his own life if he could not see his beloved daughter again. His life was not worth living without her, he wrote, his even hand not the hand of a man facing trial for the worst abuse of all.

"Alison must have got the letter yesterday," Jeanne said. "She was a bit distraught when she came home from school. Said that the maths teacher gave out to her because her homework wasn't up to scratch. So I left it. She'd always been a sensitive girl, every little incident at school upset her and I saw no point in pushing it. How I wish I had insisted. But who was to know?"

That evening Alison went out for a walk with Sandra, the girl who shared her room at Jeanne's. They walked for half an hour. When they came back, Alison went up to their room, saying she was tired.

"I noticed she hadn't done much homework and asked her about it. She shrugged. 'What does it matter anyhow?' she said, her voice smaller than usual. 'Soon I'll have that baby and who cares about exams then?' 'You do care about exams, my girl,' I said as sternly and lovingly as I could. But Alison shrugged again and went upstairs. When I went up later to

22

see how she was doing, she was sitting at her desk writing. I presumed she'd decided to do her work after all so I let her be. What she was doing was writing this letter." Jeanne pushed a hastily-written letter on lined school paper into my hand.

"Dear Jeanne and Tony," I read. "Today I realised, finally, that I can't continue to live. I'm sorry about the little baby, he or she won't have a chance. Never mind. Better to have one less child doomed to be abused and destroyed. I'm also sorry about all the love you have given me, now it is all wasted. There's no point in staying in this world. I have too much pain, too much badness in me, too much badness around me. It's not only his fault, it's also mine and Mum's. Mostly mine. I allowed him to do it to me day after day. Year after year. I feel no fear, no anger now. I feel only a strange peace, now that I've decided to do what I'm doing. I'm sorry only about the mess you will have to clear and about having to deal with all the stupid journalists. They won't let me die in peace. They have never let me live in peace. But I'm sorry, there's no other way. I deserve it and he deserves it and Mum deserves it. We are all bad, rotten to the core and all your love could not save us. Alison."

By the time I finished reading, I was shaking all over. Alison was right, we never did leave her in peace. She might not have died if I hadn't insisted on ransacking her life. When will it all end, I kept thinking, shaking more vigorously, yet feeling strangely unmoved, as if it was all happening to someone else. I had never become accustomed to feeling, I realised now. Later I confessed to Jeanne that I couldn't have done the story. "I feel too guilty. I could never have filed. Did anyone from my paper come?"

"I've no idea. They come and go, asking the same

23

questions," Jeanne said. "But we aren't talking. Let the police handle it."

As soon as I got home that night, the phone rang. Without waiting to hear who it was, I said into the receiver, "OK, Don. Lay off. I need my sleep," and replaced the receiver without waiting to hear his voice.

The phone rang twice more that night but I replaced the receiver without answering as I prepared for a sleepless night. I had confused, short dreams and woke up after each of them with the face of an unshaven man in a striped, torn uniform approaching mine, baring yellowing teeth and shaking a clenched fist in my face.

I stayed in bed the following day and in the evening drove home. I asked Mother not to tell anyone I was home. "It's that girl I wrote about. She died."

Mother nodded. "Yes, I heard it on the news and wondered if it was the same girl," her voice even as always.

I spent the next forty-eight hours mostly asleep. Mother reported several phone calls from the paper and from friends, who, having heard the news, tried to get in touch and presumed I had gone home.

Mother had lived alone since Father died of a sudden heart attack four years ago. Father's exacting, Germanic attitude, and his demands that his daughter succeed in anything she tried, had put a lot of pressure on me as a child. Even now I could feel his disapproval. "Bad to leave things in the middle, Patricia," I could hear his voice. "You should have seen this story to its end. Never let your emotions rule your decisions." Something inside me too admonished me for shirking my responsibility. At the same time I kept reliving the adolescent arguments I used to have with Father.

How can you, after the camps, adopt such a Germanic point of view, I would laugh in his face. Father would get very angry. What do you know about Germanic, he would shout across the dark, polished dining-table. The Nazis were monsters, but there were many decent Germans. We were decent Germans. And much did it help you, I would throw back at him. There is little point in blaming German values and German decency for those monsters, Father would say, his face red. And Mother would hush him. Leave it, Erich, no point in upsetting yourself. Patricia is only a teenager. You know what that means. But Father would leave the table mumbling something about the youth of today. Yet he never talked to me about those days, his silence echoing between us like a glass wall as far as memory stretched.

The story did appear on Sunday, with Seán and Orla's bylines. Much of it was composed of my back copy. And the voice inside said, Father was right. You should have seen this through. But all the time the fear strangled, like fingers round my neck.

I sat in Mother's living-room on Sunday morning sipping China tea and reading all the Sunday papers without curiosity. The Alison who emerged from the reports was not the Alison I had known, bright, intelligent, hurt. The photographs, mostly old shots taken at the time of my initial story, showed a blurred image of an average schoolgirl. Awkward. And painfully young.

Later that Sunday, Marianne rang from London. Mother covered the mouthpiece with her hand and asked if I wanted to talk to her. As I went to the phone, I knew I had to leave Ireland to make the pain go away.

"Someone just brought around your paper," Marianne said. "How terrible. Poor girl."

"Yes. Marianne, can I come and stay with you for a while?"

"What's the matter, Patricia?"

"I don't know. I've had a terrible shock. I've got to get away from here," I said quietly, glancing at Mother to check if she heard.

Mother did not appear to be listening. "Congratulations, Patricia," Marianne said. "Pity it had to take this poor creature's death for you to realise you have to get away."

When I came off the phone, having arranged with Marianne to arrive the following week, Mother came to sit beside me on the sofa. "What was it that you were talking about, Patricia?" she asked gently.

"I suppose I might as well tell you. Remember the fellow who used to phone me here all the time?"

"He phoned three or four times since you arrived and grilled me," Mother said. "'Are you sure she hasn't been in touch? Aren't you worried about her? I'm her news editor, you know, and we're all very worried.'"

"Bugger," I said angrily. "What did you say? Typical him, trying to scare you into giving him information."

"I said you phoned and said you were going away for a few days to rest, that you were very upset and that I wasn't worried, now that I knew you were taking time off." Mother smiled wryly.

"Well done, Mother." I took a deep breath. "That fellow and I have been having an affair."

"So?" Mother said, giving away no emotions.

"So nothing. Only that he's married and has three daughters. Which is why I never wanted you to meet him."

"Oh dear," Mother said. "What a mess. You could have told me. I wouldn't have shot you."

26

I looked into Mother's eyes. She had been an authoritative mother, but quiet, undemonstrative. Always agreeing with her strict husband. Never voicing her own opinion. Yet she kept herself separate. Sealed. I didn't really know that woman. What was behind her composed Germanic exterior? How had her past shaped her? I remembered her long silences, lasting weeks at times. Her stony, obstinate expressions as she sat for hours in the semi-dark living-room. Only recently had I begun to wonder what she made of the strange country she found herself in when they came to the Dublin of the early 1950s, after the camp. I now asked for the first time.

"It was, how do you call it, a culture shock." Mother's face was almost expressionless. "It was a country of peasants when we came. There was nothing European about it. It took a couple of years, but eventually they allowed us in. And let your father practice. Which was more than other countries did. And they left us alone here. No open anti-semitism. Not like England. The British didn't like our German name, and German accents. We went there first, you know. We were lucky, I suppose. After a few years there we got British citizenship, and only then were we allowed here. They didn't take many Jews here, you know. They took no Jews at all during the war. But we were never ridiculed here. Only a few jokes here and there. Which was why we decided to keep ourselves to ourselves and didn't join the Jewish establishment."

"I often wondered why you didn't bring me up as a Jew," I said quietly. "Calling me Patricia, of all names."

"This had been our way of being Jewish in Frankfurt too. Most of our friends were not Jewish. We never went to Temple. Yet we were proud Jews. And when the time came, it made no difference. They took everyone. Those who went to Temple and people like us. People, our friends, kept saying it would never happen. They wouldn't touch Jewish doctors. They respected us too much. But you know what Jewish doctors ended up doing in the camps. Mind you, it was being a doctor which saved your father from the gas. And me, what saved me was being young and strong, a good worker."

"You never talked about it," I said, looking at Mother, suddenly frail in her dusky pink angora sweater.

"No. Your father didn't want to talk about it. Ironically, he loved Germany too much." Mother sighed. "He couldn't bear to think that his cultured Germany could have done this to us."

"And why did you wait to long to have a child?" I asked.

"Wait so long?" Mother said, pain passing over her face like rain-clouds. "We didn't wait that long." She paused and looked at me. "We had a little daughter. Hanna."

Mother pronounced the name like a prayer. I felt a hand tighten on my throat. Hanna? They'd never said. Mother looked out the window and continued. "We had some hours before they took us away. We asked our friends, the Magdenburgs, to take her. She was blond. Had blue eyes. Could pass for German. They said they would change her name. They had always loved her."

"And what happened to her?" I asked almost inaudibly.

Mother's face went into a thousand little wrinkles, as if she was going to cry. She didn't. She never had. Instead she looked vacantly ahead of her and continued very slowly. "When we came out, we spent a long time in transit camps, looking for each other. Like everyone else we were hungry. Brutalised by having survived. And guilty. That guilt has

28

never left me." She paused again, her stare blank. "It took us months to locate each other and months to get used to living again. The transit camps were almost as bad. No, no, what am I saying? But it was tough. We almost didn't dare to say her name. It took more time before we could say to each other let's look for Hanna. It was endless. We tried to locate our friends in Frankfurt but couldn't. Their street was bombed and no one knew where they were. He stayed in town. Was not taken into the army because his speciality was needed to treat wounded soldiers. But despite the famous German order and precision, we never found them. Two years after the war ended, we found their names in a casualty list and presumed our girl had died too in one of the air raids. But we never traced her name on any list. Did they die because of her? Did she die because we left her behind?" Mother's voice trailed off. She sighed lightly. "There isn't a day I don't think of it, you know."

"But Mother." I searched her eyes. "You never said."

"No. We made a decision never to talk about it. Not even to each other. Only at night. We would wake each other up from nightmares, shouting her name."

I shuddered. Two days ago I had no dead. Only Father. Now I had Alison. And Hanna.

"We travelled across Europe," Mother continued, speaking each word with great effort now. "Eventually we got to England and then here. It took such a long time. Your father didn't want to have any more children. This is not a world fit for children, he used to say. And I was too frightened to remind him of all our dead. Our brothers and sisters and the children they could have had. And of Hanna."

She signed and talked on. "When I did become pregnant, I was almost forty-five. I had started my menopause and stopped taking precautions. Didn't think I could become pregnant again. But I was so happy I decided I was going to fight him if he refused to let me have it. Have you. But to my surprise, he was happy too. Up until then he made me take precautions all the time. It wasn't always easy to get contraception here in Ireland, but because he was a doctor he managed. It was an accident, really. But he saw it as an omen. Somebody up there wants us to have a child, he said the night I told him in trepidation. He opened a bottle of French champagne and drank it all himself. Didn't let me touch a drop during my pregnancy. And the rest you know."

"And Patricia?"

"This was his way of thanking Ireland for taking us in. He loved you more than his life. Wanted only the best for you. Sometimes I feared he considered you his compensation. For everything we lost."

"But he criticised me for all he was worth."

"Because he wanted you to have everything, can't you see?"

"I can see it now. But it wasn't always easy at the time. I carry it with me until now."

"Don't, child," Mother said. "Let him go. Let him rest in peace. Look at me, almost seventy and I am still carrying my father in my head. His religious obsessions. You should have married a religious man, become a good Jewish wife, was all he said after the wedding. But he too perished. Much good did his God do him."

I looked at Mother. Her hair, still not completely grey, combed neatly in an old-fashioned bun, a hairstyle she had had ever since I could remember. Her skin taut, her pain never showed, perhaps only in the long silences, only in the eyes which never shone. This pain is probably what happened to me. What made me so scared.

I didn't ask any more questions. Gaining a dead sister was enough for one day. I felt immobilised by the dead weight Mother had just burdened me with. But I realised now I had always carried that weight, always unknowingly struggled uphill, carrying my pain around my neck.

When I told Mother an hour later I had decided to leave Don, I realised I hadn't asked what I needed to know about Hanna. I would ask her another day, I thought, knowing I wouldn't. Instead I said, "I've tried to leave him several times, particularly since I met that girl, Alison. But he always talks me back. But not this time. I'm not going back."

"And your job?" Mother asked softly, as if nothing else had been said between us.

"I don't know yet. I have some holidays coming, I'm going to spend a week with Marianne and then I'll have to face the music, I suppose. But by then I may be better able to make a decision."

Mother hugged me lightly, holding me stiffly close to her chest. I could not remember ever being held by Mother, who now patted my neck and shoulders, rocking me like a forlorn baby.

Marianne, no longer the shy girl she had been before going to London, took me to a women's support group she belonged to, where I met a mixed group of women, all of whom had been in long-term destructive relationships. The group leader was Miri, a sallow-skinned Israeli, who had come to London in order to break a nine-year long affair with a married man. She was bright and outspoken, yet kind and supportive as each woman took turns to talk to the group. Many cried as they spoke, others shouted and shook, and each time Miri encouraged them to cry more, shake more.

When it was my turn, I didn't find it hard to tell my story. I told this group of strangers things I had never told anyone. Realising I had been too busy looking tough and in control to admit I was in pain. No one interrupted. The women listened attentively, delighting in my "emergence," as they kept telling me later. Marianne sat very close, holding my hand as I spoke of my newly-found, lost sister, about lost, dead Alison, about Don. I had never thought I could relate this to anyone and when I finished, I felt exhausted. I spent the night talking to Miri and Marianne. It was nothing Miri said, but at the end of the night, I decided I would like to go to Israel.

"It could be some things Mother said last week. About the camps. About losing their daughter. My sister. Hanna. They never said. I find it hard to say the words 'my sister.' Something broke inside me when she told me. So soon after Alison's death. Do you know I was never inside a synagogue in Dublin?" I was speaking fast, breathlessly. "The only Judaism I encountered was in Marianne's house. Yet my parents were so Jewish. So different from anyone else. Does it make sense?"

By the end of the week I had a plan. I was going to Israel to interview Israeli and Palestinian women for a book. I rehearsed my strategy with Marianne. I would not confront Don but go straight to the editor whom I would ask for three months' leave. I would also ask him to commission me to file copy. "They can hardly refuse you, their star reporter," Marianne said.

On my first day back, I was called for an urgent news

32

conference in Don's office and was assigned to cover a hospital strike. A third-rate story. But I agreed without argument. To pass the time until I left.

When the conference was over, Don asked me to stay. He closed the door and said quietly. "Where bloody were you? I was looking for you everywhere. Even phoned your friend in London, Marianne, who said she hadn't heard from you in months."

"Good old Marianne, knew I could trust her. I actually spent the week with her."

"Why are you doing this to me, Patsy?" Don said, his voice very controlled.

"I don't wish to be called Patsy any more. You can call me Pat, or Patricia."

My voice made him recoil. "We can discuss it tonight, can't we?" and his voice started to caress me as his eyes moved along my body, hungry.

"There is nothing to discuss," I said. "Tonight or any other night."

I turned to go and Don didn't stop me. I headed straight to the editor's office and came out with three months' leave and a commission for a weekly dispatch.

When I came home that evening, Don was waiting outside my front door with a bunch of red carnations.

I walked past him and almost pushed him out of my way. He was not coming in. I knew he might talk me into sex if he made his way in. We argued in muffled voices outside my front door. After some time, Don realised he was losing and left.

That night the phone rang several times, but each time I lifted the receiver and replaced it immediately. I slept soundly for the first time since Alison's death.

Night was falling and the windows had darkened over the frothy clouds as the stewardesses served the meal. I put on the earphones and listened to the Israeli Phil playing Beethoven. As the lights dimmed, I curled in the narrow space, the earphones around my neck.

What am I doing running away like this. Why am I going so far. If anyone should go, he should. Take his precious family and go away from me, out of my life. But it is never like this. They never lose. The anger I felt drowned the other voice, of self-blame. I knew it wasn't Don I was running away from. It wasn't even Alison. I was running to something. Starting a long search which began when Mother told me about Hanna. Where did I go wrong? Such success, they all say. Such brilliance. Never leave unfinished work. Never let your emotions rule. Where did I go wrong?

CHAPTER TWO

An old Arab sat stonily on a low fence in the pale Hebron dawn. How does he feel about all this activity, I thought, as soldiers ran in and out of my vision, shouting sharp commands and holding submachine-guns at what seemed like a menacing angle, if you discounted their teenage faces.

"Ask him," I said to the young lieutenant who was seconded from the Army Spokesman's office to accompany me, "what he is thinking while all this is going on."

The officer, a solicitor in civilian life, smiled benignly as if questioning my reason, but said nothing. He then addressed the old Arab in what sounded like school Arabic. The old man lifted a furrowed brow towards the young officer, his face surprisingly calm, and spoke slowly.

"He says he's seen it all before," Lieutenant Avi said. "The Turks have come and gone, the British have come and gone, the Israelis have come and they'll go."

"And what do you think yourself?" I asked Avi, courtesy itself, unusual in this country where everyone seemed to be living on the edge of their nerves.

"I think it's an understandable point of view," Avi said in his patient American accent.

"Come off it, Avi, you can do better than that. I've seen it all in Northern Ireland. Everywhere there is this kind of war,

35

there are old men sitting on fences and saying it will all come to pass. But it doesn't mean that soldiers like what these old men say. So what do you really think, Avi?"

"What I think has little to do with it," Avi said. "I'm on duty and my job is to give you the information you need and take you wherever you want to go, which is unusual in itself. Most journalists don't bother with us, you know. They make their own way and get their information from the locals."

"I really want to know what you think, Avi," I had already noticed the tendency of Israelis to make statements and I wasn't going to let this go.

"OK, you win," Avi smiled. "What I really want is for this reserve service to be over as soon as possible. I've two more days and I'm dying to get back to the practice. It's costing me a fortune. And it's also a hell of a price to pay for having returned from the US. Satisfied?"

I was taken aback. After only a week, I already felt embroiled in the intricacies of the place. I did know that every Israeli male was required to serve several weeks each year as an army reservist but I haven't yet talked to anyone about the hardship of serving. Up to now, I'd been busy establishing contacts and witnessing the harassment of Palestinians. The *intifada* was taking its toll not only in precious young lives but also economically. I hadn't given much thought to the price Israelis were paying. This despite the Palestinians' triumphalism when talking of the success of the *intifada*. To my surprise, all this made me feel guilty. You live in safe, grey old Ireland while young Israelis and Palestinians fight over this place.

"Satisfied?" I was trying to keep my tone light, not reveal my guilt. "No. What you've just said was that you're fed up, but you didn't say what you thought of what the old man said,

36

that it's only a matter of time before you're defeated." And all the time I was also thinking how to turn all this into effective copy for my first report. Avoiding the real issue.

"This old man is right and he isn't right. In global historical terms, he may be right. Their population is increasing while our birth rate is falling. They're becoming more and more determined to capture the world's imagination and defeat us with a clever combination of public relations and this persistent uprising. It's dogged, it's using effective weapons such as women and children. And we can't win, however hard we come down on them. On the other hand, there's our determination not to leave this land, the only Jewish state in the whole world. And our determination that it will never happen again. Whatever 'it' may be, the Holocaust, the pogroms, the inquisition, the destruction of the temple, you name it. Our determination will keep us here as obstinately as Palestinian attachment to the land will keep them here."

As soldiers passed behind Avi's back, running heavily up the little hill towards the town centre, I reflected that what I'd heard from this smooth Americanised Israeli was a summary of the Israeli Palestinian conflict.

"Now, if you have no other questions, perhaps you'd like to move on. I think things are going to hot up in a couple of moments. I've just heard on the radio that a band of youngsters have prepared us a little surprise down the lane," Avi said, barely disguising a smile.

"Shit, Avi, you've just given me perfect copy for my article. Sure, I want to see a piece of the action. And remember, I'm seeing it courtesy of the Israel Defence Forces, not through the enemy's eyes." I chuckled, but Avi remained serious.

He talked into his radio in Hebrew and said, "OK, get into the jeep. I've got special permission to let you join in. But be warned," he said quickly, "this may be dangerous. I hope your paper covers bringing your remains back home."

I had no time to answer. I was hurled into a jeep which started moving behind the soldiers walking slowly along the sleepy lane. "They're already up, they've prepared us a dawn chorus," Avi said as the jeep moved bumpily on the rough road. "Usually they wait for the light, wait for us to have our breakfast. This is a new departure."

As he spoke, the voices coming through the radio became louder and faster. When the jeep braked suddenly, I caught a glimpse of Avi's submachine-gun jerking out of the passenger window. In front of the jeep, two groups of soldiers on both sides of the lane stood staring into a bonfire. Masses of black smoke filled the air with an appalling stench, the likes of which I remembered from trips to Derry and Belfast. Burnt rubber, the smell of anger and hatred.

Behind the smoke, several youths stood, their faces covered in grey and white kaffiyehs, their dark eyes menacing. Suddenly, a movement among the soldiers. A large cement block was dropped from one of the roofs. I could see a small figure, a child, hurrying back along the flat roof. Then more missiles. "Shit," Avi said. "Literally. They've taken to throwing plastic bags filled with shit and piss."

I shuddered. And then smiled. Clever sods. But I felt for the soldiers too. Children. But then the other side were also so young. Their hatred maturing them into menacing men. Confusing. As I was writing my copy in my head, reluctant to take out a notebook for fear I would miss something, my thoughts raced, my feelings jumbled. Missiles were flying everywhere now. And shouts sounding like curses. In Hebrew.

"They speak Hebrew?"

"Enough to curse the soldiers, their mothers, their sisters and their fathers," Avi laughed. "Enough to make the soldiers lose their cool."

The soldiers, who up to now had been standing erect under the jutting roofs, were starting to show signs of impatience. "Not allowed to shoot, until in danger," Avi explained. "But it won't take long."

A single shot. Several missiles were hurled at once and arms were flailing. The youths scattered and then returned with bags of stones which they hurled at the soldiers. One of the soldiers caught a youth from behind the smoke and pulled him forward. Shouts, and suddenly a scrumlike heap of khaki descended on the youth as batons and limbs seemed to fly in all directions.

"Leave the poor bugger alone," the jeep's driver screamed suddenly in English as he left his seat to walk towards the scrummy mass. He shouted in Hebrew but no one heeded. He moved to reason with the remaining soldiers who were eyeing the now distant youths. One waved him aside. He persisted and then an officer approached, who seemed to listen and shouted a brief command.

The end was as fast as the beginning and as sudden. The scrum subsided and the soldiers returned to their formation, shaking dust off their crumpled uniforms. The beaten youth lay limp on the grey road. His colleagues approached gingerly to look. They talked quietly to each other and as a taxi approached, they lifted their friend carefully on to the back seat.

"What happens to him now?"

"He will be taken to one of their hospitals," Avi said. "If he's lucky, he'll have connections in one of the private hospitals. Government hospitals don't treat *intifada* victims. This isn't what we fund them for. But they often manage to get in, claiming their injuries were caused by a family brawl."

"Poor devil," the driver said."What was that all about?"

"God knows, seems to have started from nothing," Avi agreed.

"Can you find out for me what exactly happened there? I'll need it for my report."

"You're lucky. You saw a real *intifada* incident, without having to pay some local youths to throw stones for you, as so many foreign journalists do," Avi said. "I'll try and get you the official version."

The youths dispersed, like travelling actors having given an ancient ritual performance everyone knows by heart. The soldiers remained in lines, preparing to proceed and comb the narrow lanes until dusk. Avi left the jeep and returned after several minutes with a dark man in civics whom he introduced as Colonel Daniel. "This is Patricia Goldman from Dublin, Ireland," he said in English. "She would like the official explanation of what happened here."

Colonel Daniel looked me straight in the eye. He had amazingly light blue eyes for such a dark face and something in his hard stare made me recoil.

"We were looking for an important leader, following a tip we received last night. The blockade was meant to divert our attention," he said. "The locals were cursing our boys. How long do you think these boys can stand it? One of them lost his cool and, because of the order not to shoot, decided to simply beat one up. That's the whole story."

"Simply beat one up?" I repeated. "You mean, like what your Minister of Defence said some months ago?"

"I'm only a soldier, I don't know about politics. You should ask our friend here from the army spokesman's office policy questions," Daniel said, his voice harsh. And all the while I felt uncomfortable, his stare did not leave my face.

"How about returning to Jerusalem?" Avi said. "Do you have enough information for your article?"

"Sure." I'd had enough official Israeli information. I wanted to go back to Jerusalem and talk to the East Jerusalem Palestine Information Centre. It was Thursday and I had to file copy that night or at the latest the next morning.

"Do you have time for breakfast in my hotel?" I asked the three men and no one in particular.

"Where are you staying?" Avi asked.

Before I could answer, Daniel said firmly, "Ariel."

I was going to ask how he knew, but the driver, Uri, spoke first. "Our friends in the *Shin Bet* know more about you than you know about yourself, Patricia. Get used to it. This is Israel."

"I won't be joining you," Daniel said. "My working day has just begun."

"Cheerio, then, comrade Colonel," Uri said. "See you around when I next serve in this godforsaken shithouse, if I don't decide to be a territories refusenik, that is."

"And rot in the special pink liberal prison wing?" Daniel asked, without awaiting a reply. Uri was already busy starting the jeep's engine, urging Avi to get in. Daniel said slowly, his light eyes searching my face, "Bye, Patricia, see you around."

I had been in Israel only a week, but much had happened to sharpen my sense of belonging and alienation.

The bus trip from the airport into Tel Aviv in the early

morning was disappointing. Approaching the Tel Aviv central bus station as businesses started opening, I was appalled by the squalor and neglect. Peeling plaster, narrow streets, street vendors preparing their wares for the day's business. It all looked more like an Arab town than like Israel's newest city, built on the sands earlier this century.

Things improved as the first morning bus travelled towards Jerusalem. The hilly carriageway to Jerusalem was lined with green pine forests. The entrance to Jerusalem, the built-up surrounding hills, the broad roads exuded calm after Tel Aviv's early-morning chaos.

I had been given explicit instructions to phone a friend of Miri's when I arrived in Jerusalem. It was not yet eight o'clock when I got to Jerusalem and I hesitated to call, although Israel seemed fully awake. When I finally called, Miri's friend, Nava greeted me cheerfully and suggested a meeting later that day. She gave me several names of hotels and promised to look for a place for me to stay as soon as she could manage it. Even on the phone, I was overwhelmed by Israeli hospitality, drawing me in on my first day.

The first hotel I called, the Ariel, it faced the old city walls, which glistened in the yellow morning sun. I unpacked and strolled towards the city, past flowering parks, the golden dome of the Holy Sepulchre sparkling to my right.

The first few hours shattered the mental pictures I had built of Israel. Order, cleanliness and much greenery vied with dust and dirt. It was Jerusalem's modernity which struck me. I'd expected an ancient eastern metropolis.

The first week passed as if in a dream. Between making contacts, arranging interviews, getting press accreditation and being accompanied to the West Bank by Lieutenant Avi to get material for my first dispatch, I had little time for

42

reflection. The dry Jerusalem spring heat, the magical evening light and above all, the intensity of the people I met through Nava enveloped me in a clear white haze. Don receded into a foggy background and his telephone calls failed to arouse any feelings. My body still ached for his. His voice on the phone seemed as close as if he was speaking from the next room, but my mind floated, detached.

At night I lay awake in my hotel room, trying to remember Alison and the fear, but very little came. Here, where young men and women were combating in deadly seriousness the likes of which I had encountered in the North and in South Africa, child abuse seemed remote. Alison, I realised with alarm, was taking a back seat in my mind. Hanna, on the other hand, was continually in my thoughts. I eyed every blond woman I saw in the street obsessively. Why are you expecting to find her here? She died, poor child. Another one of your dead. Father. Alison. And now Hanna.

I got more embroiled in the business of being a Middle East correspondent. The recent past pushed into the dark recesses of my memory.

Don called after I had faxed my first dispatch. "Bloody marvellous, Patsy," his voice rang. "You got so much passion into the piece. And your comparison with the North. It'll make them sit up."

"Thanks, Don," I tried to sound casual. "It was easy. Copy here writes itself. Events are stronger than words."

"Easy, ha?" Don said. "I wish other things were easy for you too, like coming back to me."

"Leave off, Don. You know why I'm here."

"I'll never leave off," Don said. "Hold on a minute," his voice changed, "OK, I'm coming, tell him I'll be with him in a couple of seconds," he was obviously talking to someone else. "When will you be back in the hotel?"

"I don't know. You'd better not call that often."

"Nonsense, girl. When will you be there?"

"I don't know. I'm off now to meet some women for my book. It's the sabbath here tomorrow and everything shuts from this afternoon on, so I may be out for the weekend."

"I'll catch you sometime. Watch out for these randy Airabs," Don said, his tone lighter, "and get me another strong piece for next week."

Blast him, why won't he leave me in peace, I thought as the phone rang again. I picked up the receiver and a man's voice on the other end said gingerly, "Miss Goldman?"

"Yes, who is it?"

"Abed Touquan, a friend of Nava's. Can we have coffee?"

"Where are you?" I wasn't ready. I was looking forward to spending the quiet Friday afternoon strolling around Jerusalem which was assuming a spiritual mantle, as everything closed for the approaching sabbath. The skies echoed a golden light on the biscuit-coloured old city walls. Later that night I was invited to meet a group of Nava's friends.

"In your hotel lobby. But I have a car, we can go somewhere else if you want," Abed's impeccably British voice said.

I got into my jeans quickly. I was beginning to get used to things changing fast here. The man who was waiting for me in the lobby wore a well-tailored navy suit, the kind ordinary Israelis did not wear. He was slight and his shiny black hair glistened. "Thank you for coming," he said, extending his hand and smiling. "Nava said you wanted to talk to someone from the university. I teach sociology at Bir Zeit and I thought I could help you."

"Pleased to meet you." I squeezed his dry warm hand.

"Where would you like to go?" he asked. "I can take you to a coffee house in East Jerusalem. If you're not afraid, that is?"

I had already been to East Jerusalem, to the Palestine Information Centre. I still felt nervous about it, but there was no polite way of refusing.

Abed Touquan's charm equalled Avi's desperate wish to please at all times. He did not court me, yet his eyes seemed to compliment me all through our conversation. We sat opposite Jaffa Gate in a small tiled coffeehouse over endless cups of Turkish coffee which kept reappearing until I had to ask Touquan to stop their flow. I was introduced to the intricacies of West Bank universities, their closure by the military government and the clandestine ways in which students continued to pursue their studies. When he got to the women he proposed I interview for the book, I had to ask why I was meeting him and not one of the women.

"Most are under house arrest," he said simply.

I froze. "House arrest? For being women?"

"You can say that." Touquan smiled patiently. "The *intifada* brought women and children to the fore. The men are obvious targets. But most Israeli soldiers find it hard to shoot or beat women and children, although they find other ways. Like putting women activists under house arrest."

"Don't you think that putting women and children on the streets is unfair?" I asked, although this was the way in the North. The rioting men get arrested or hide and the women and children take over.

Abed Touquan seemed to have read my thoughts. "You are from Ireland, aren't you, Miss Goldman? And from your name I presume you are Jewish?"

"Yes, but what's the connection?" His patronising tone irritated me.

"You must know that in popular uprisings like ours, against a well-equipped army, we have little choice of soldiers or tactics," he said. I said nothing, waiting for the second part of his argument. "You know that, because you're an experienced news reporter, I'm told. But as a Jew you have a problem with it, haven't you?"

"As a Jew I'm not worth much." I was beginning to warm to this man. "I'm afraid I'm not a practicing Jew. My parents weren't religious before the war and the camps didn't convince them. So they brought me up in a predominantly Catholic country without any religion. I went to a convent school, and I mixed with non-Jews. So I've no qualms about it as a Jew, only as a human being and, dare I say it, as a feminist." It was the first time I had used the term to define myself.

"You'll have plenty of opportunities to discuss all this with the women we want you to meet," Touquan said. He ignored the comments about the camp. Perhaps he didn't want to have to cope with it. "They're all feminists. And believe me, being a feminist in Arab society isn't easy."

I was amazed by his vehemence. "What's your own angle on that? You're a man, after all."

He smiled. "I think you're beginning to find out that things here are not as they seem," he said. "Arab society and Arab men are extremely traditional. I was brought up in such ways. But since I was educated in Britain and since my wife is an American Palestinian, I'm trying to live my life differently. I share the views of the women you'll meet that there's little point in having a Palestinian state which oppresses half its population. But let's have a Palestinian state first and then we'll get everything else right."

46

"That's what they all say. In Northern Ireland, in Algeria, in South Africa, everywhere. But you know it doesn't work. You've to get it all right at the same go and establish precedents before you have a state."

"Which is why these women have chosen to be in the front line of the *intifada*," Abed could not resist a little triumphant smile. "But we can't afford the luxury of waiting until everything is right," he argued. "There's a war on here. We are under occupation and we have figured out the only way we know to break the deadlock and force our occupiers to give us what we want, a state of our own. A peaceful uprising by unarmed citizens, men, women and children."

I was suddenly conscious of my painless transition to the feminist argument, which I had resisted for so long. Until Alison. I was getting used to everybody here making political speeches at every opportunity, Israelis and Palestinians alike. "Don't you people ever tire of the everlasting politics?"

"My answer must remain the same," Abed smiled again. "We can't afford the luxury. The personal is political, as you feminists say. We must find a solution, sooner rather than later."

I liked Abed Touquan, despite his patronising tone. If this was to be the new Palestinian man, there was hope for Palestinian womanhood, I thought. "You'll find more and more Palestinian men, certainly in Ramallah and Jerusalem, relinquishing the old mode of thinking," he said, as if reading my thoughts. "You can attend political meetings in private houses where women make the speeches and men look after the babies. So perhaps things are changing."

We parted at the hotel after Abed had promised to set up a meeting early the following week.

47

Israel was beginning to grow on me. You could certainly not remain indifferent here. As I strolled down the street in the fading evening light, I breathed the dry cool Jerusalem air and my excitement grew.

The phone rang as I entered the room. Don sounded more remote than ever. "How is my girl?"

"I'm not your girl and I'm great."

"Come, come," Don said. "What's the matter?" From his voice I could tell he had had a few drinks.

"Nothing is the matter. On the contrary. I'm having a great time and I don't feel like talking to you until this time next week when I send my next article."

"Oh, don't you now?" Don's voice mocked. "And what if I told you that unless you're nice to me, we won't use your copy?"

"Then I'll go straight to Mike. My contract is with him. You're jarred, Don, why don't you go home?"

"Aren't we the hard lady?" Don's slurred words angered me.

"I'm going to put the phone down now, Don," I kept my voice even. "I'll talk to you again next Thursday, when I fax my copy. Have a good weekend."

I replaced the receiver. Don had hooked me from the start, I reflected, made me want him. And from the start I had made the choice of going along with him. But now was the time for different choices. Time to suit myself. I telephoned the switchboard and told them not to pass on any calls from Don. With this done, I felt lighter. I spent the rest of the evening bathing and resting, thinking about the past week.

Nava lived not far from the hotel in an old Arab house which, she was at pains to explain, was not classified as

48

deserted Arab property invaded by Jews after the 1948 victory. "This house here," she said as I admired the arched living-room littered with oriental ornaments, "was Arab built but, like so many houses in the German Colony, it belonged to the Templars, German settlers who settled in Erez Israel, hoping to bring about the return of the Messiah by encouraging the Jews to return to their Biblical homeland."

Nava's other guests, who started gathering soon after I arrived, were all of a similar political conviction. It was an academic crowd, typical, I would learn later, of a free-thinking element in Israeli society. Not politically affiliated to any of the major alignments, they voted for the liberal left-of-centre small parties, signed petitions for human rights and went on Peace Now demonstrations. But they joined solidarity groups with West Bank detainees and, above all, they didn't refuse reserve service in the territories, believing that their presence there mitigated possible atrocities.

The conversation was fast, the guests often resorted to Hebrew and came back to English only when Nava chided them. Drinking bottled Israeli beer and chilled Israeli wine and munching pistachio nuts, olives and savoury pastries, they talked mostly about the *intifada* and the government's stupidity or brutality, depending on who was speaking.

They were all curious about me. Nava, who had spent her childhood in England, found it strange that my parents gave me no Jewish education, particularly after having lost all their family in the Holocaust.

"I can understand it," said Amos, a senior law lecturer at the Hebrew University and a well-known human rights activist. "Like my parents, they were probably cosmopolitan German Jews. Mine had the foresight to get out in time. But they were outraged by what was done in the name of their cultured Germany. They actually wanted to go to the States, not here. It took them years to get used to living here and to this day they rant and rave against this place. Primitive, they call it, Asiatic. And they don't celebrate any Jewish holidays, not even Passover. They won't even go to synagogue on Yom Kippur, for God's sake. And I had a hard time convincing them I wanted to have a Barmitzvah like all the other boys."

"Still, it's unusual, you must admit," said Rina, a dark-haired petite paediatrician. "Bringing up a kid in a Catholic country and not giving her any notion of her Jewish heritage."

"It's pretty weird," I agreed, "particularly since Ireland is so obsessed with religion. But I've never challenged them about it. That was the way it was and I realised early on in life that every family has its peculiarities."

"And yet you find yourself here," said Amos' wife, Dalia. "Why here of all places?"

"Come off it, Dalia," Nava said protectively. "It's an unfair question."

"No, it isn't," I said. With these people, whose curiosity and directness was unlike anything I had ever experienced, I could speak openly. "I had a personal crisis. Alison, a girl I was writing about, a child abuse case, killed herself. I was shattered. I went home to Mother. For comfort. We talked and suddenly she comes out with a story about a daughter they once had. Before the camps. They gave her to a German couple. To save her. And the three of them disappeared. On top of all this, my personal life was in a mess. I needed a reason to get out of Ireland. I could have gone to London or applied for a US visa, but I happened to meet Nava's friend Miri in London and she gave me the idea of coming here to write a book about women. So I thought I could use the time

50

to find out about being Jewish. And perhaps find out about Hanna too. A wild-goose chase, I'm sure. So here I am. And funnily, although I am here only a week, it's already starting to feel like coming home."

Nava's friends looked at me as I spoke. Some averted their gaze when I mentioned Hanna. The pain here was too near the surface. No one said anything, so I went on to tell them about meeting Abed Touquan whom some of them knew through the Human Rights League. "He's a good man," Amos said. "Has his head screwed on. Unlike some of them."

"What do you mean by that?" asked Rachel, a journalist with the country's main evening paper.

"Oh, sorry, Rachel, didn't mean to hurt your feelings," Amos said mockingly. "Rachel here cannot hear a bad word said about Arabs," he added. "Nonsense," Rachel said. She was the most politically extreme of Nava's friends. Involved in a clandestine pro-Palestinian publication, she was outspoken and fearless. "I'd like you to qualify your statement."

"I've met some rather unsavoury characters in the territories, Rachel, as you well know," Amos said. "The trouble with so many of them is that they find it hard to talk directly. They have a deep need to please and be nice but say the opposite behind your back."

"Wouldn't you do the same in their place?" Rachel asked. "I'm sure our ancestors in the diaspora felt they had to smooth-talk their way under alien rule."

"OK, Rachel, I know it isn't easy," Amos said. "But your love of humanity, as long as it's Arab, is stupid. Like all generalisations."

"I never said they were all wonderful," Rachel said. "But

we must make allowances. They've been under occupation for such a long time."

"Which is why Abed is a great guy," Amos said. "Despite the difficulties of living under our crude occupation, he manages to retain an open mind."

"The question is not that he manages to retain a fairness, but whether we do," said Rina's husband, Gideon. "I must admit I'm with Rachel on this one. We demand too much of them, just like the world demands of us. Passing judgement on the two opposing camps here, expecting us to behave like the British."

"Don't even mention British fairness to me," I said. "There's little difference between what's going on in Northern Ireland and here, let me assure you. I've just written an article about this."

"So it had better be true," Rachel laughed. "I don't know much about the British in Northern Ireland but, believe you me, politicians and editors here are very fond of making comparisons. As if comparisons with Belfast can excuse what's going on here."

I liked Nava's friends. Their way of expressing conflicting views and arguing with one another was refreshing. In Ireland similar conversations harboured a lot of self-hatred and mockery and a lot of blame of others, the government, the Brits, anything but themselves. I asked the gathering to help me find suitable Israeli women for the book, but I found it hard to define what I was looking for.

"I sense that Israel is a complex, uneven society and I'd like the book to reflect this. I'd like to examine women's attitudes to living in a state of war, with a weak economy, with husbands who have to serve in the army every so often, with sons taken into the army to defend ideals only half the population believes in."

"You mean a society where religious Jews fight secular Jews, where advocates of the Greater Israel think that people who believe in territories for peace are traitors, where the economy stinks but where everyone lives above their means, and where the Holocaust serves as a metaphor and a daily reminder," Gideon asked.

"You can find Israeli women who'll tell you all this," Nava said, "but you'll find it very hard to get Palestinian women to reflect more than one point of view, that of the oppressed living under occupation, whose sole objective is to overthrow the regime and achieve first a Palestinian state and then a state in the whole of Palestine."

"Why?"

."They say they cannot afford the luxury of differing in public even if they have conflicting opinions on political questions," Amos offered.

"Yes, your friend Abed already said as much."

"I suggest you listen to them and then ask them why they all sound the same," Rachel said. "It'll make your book more interesting. The Israelis, who moved from being oppressed to being conquerors and occupiers, argue endlessly. They're tortured with eternal questions of morality and justice while killing the Palestinians, who moved from being oppressed to being oppressed and are getting killed in total agreement."

"You could put it differently too, Rachel," Rina said firmly. "We Jews were arguing even before we had a state, and before we became conquerors. Not only about the eternal question of Zion versus Palestine, but about everything else too, Zion versus the diaspora, for instance. Even before forty-eight we were killing each other, because we couldn't agree. The Palestinians are more determined. Perhaps they know something we have never learnt. That, in order to achieve anything, you have to concentrate your efforts and forget your differences."

"Great talkers, your friends," I said to Nava on the way back to the hotel late that night.

"Yes, Israelis are great talkers," Nava agreed. "Sometimes I think we do nothing but talk. It's easier than action. Look at the crowd you met tonight. All have their hearts in the right place. All believe in territories for peace. In journalistic shorthand you'd call us doves. But what do we do? Sign a petition every couple of months. Go to rallies. We were all there after Sabra and Shatilla. But what does it matter? While we agonise in our living-rooms on Friday nights, Palestinian kids get killed, Palestinian youths are hassled and Israeli soldiers, also kids really, get their minds twisted. And the government refuses to talk peace."

"But you do agonise."

"Oh, yes. But do we really care?" Nava asked.

"Don't think it's different elsewhere. If anything, people here care more," I said. "All my friends can say about the North is, 'Oh God, not the North again.' At least I haven't heard people here say they're bored with the situation."

"Not yet," Nava said. "It's too close to every one of us. But we too have our ways of ignoring things. We eat too much. We are compulsive shoppers. Compulsive travellers. We don't save money. We spend it as if there was no tomorrow. And perhaps there isn't."

Palestinian lecturer Najar Feidy's living-room was not unlike Nava's. An old Ramallah house with arched ceilings and oriental rugs scattered on the simple furniture.

"My study." Najar pointed to a corner of the living-room

piled high with books and papers. A map of the whole of
Palestine with a white dove hung above her desk. "When
our daughter was born, I had to give her my study. Now that
I am under house arrest, I have no choice but to work on my
thesis. I've never got so much done, thanks to the military
governor. With the university closed for the past three
months, only some of my students are allowed to take
tutorials here."

I looked into Najar's face and what I saw was not the
Arab woman I had envisaged. I found it hard to say so and,
when I did, it sounded wrong.

"What did you expect?" Najar was angry. "You
journalists fly in here and expect us to give you a folklore
show. I was educated in Lebanon and the States. I am not a
peasant although, let me tell you, it is these peasant women
who bear the brunt of the *intifada*. It is they who lose their
sons. It is they whose houses are demolished. And it is they
who carry on, strong, resilient."

"I suppose I feel embarrassed on your behalf," I tried
again.

"Don't feel embarrassed," Najar said firmly. "Our life
here is very exciting. We have a purpose. When I was in the
States, I got very involved with my students. Drug problems,
insecurity problems. Then one day I asked myself, what am I
doing here? I always knew I wanted to come back and I felt
there were thousands and thousands of Palestinians whose
problems were much more severe, more relevant. If we don't
come back here, if we don't face our problems right here, we
can't win."

I recorded Najar's answers, congratulating myself on the
lively copy Najar would make. Yet I couldn't help reflecting
that Najar too, like Lieutenant Avi, like Abed Touquan, like

Nava and her friends, was an actor playing a part in a pre-scripted pageant.

"Social depression and backwardness are part of the political backwardness," Najar said, her gaze fixed on my face, as if she was standing in front of a group of undergraduates who were hanging on her every word. "Our life may sound romantic but in reality it's victimising and discriminatory, not only against women, but against the working-class, against peasants, against the under-privileged."

"Against children?"

"Against children, definitely. Children are extremely oppressed here," she said firmly.

"Which is why you send them to the front line?"

"We don't send them," Najar said curtly. "You must understand, these children have been born under occupation. They know no other reality."

"But surely if you're going to have a free state, a free society, you would want it to be a society where women and children are no longer oppressed?"

"It's all one problem. Which is why I cannot say I won't fight for women's rights because I have a political battle to fight. It's the same fight. Of which the occupation is just an aspect."

The reverence I felt towards this powerful woman was interfering with my journalism.

"I can't tell these peasant mothers not to send their children on to the streets to throw stones at the soldiers they have been told are their enemies. But that doesn't mean I would allow my own daughter out there. I wouldn't. Not because I'm afraid for her, but because I'm a pacifist. What is the sense in getting rid of the occupation if we're still occupied by our own backwardness?"

I could hear the contradictions but found it hard to pin Najar down. Her approval of the PLO, I felt, contradicted her declared pacifism.

Najar acknowledged the contradiction. "We always feel hurt when there is an operation and people are killed, but the PLO is a political structure. Because you don't like certain actions, it doesn't mean you don't approve of the organisation as a whole."

I had heard these arguments before. Love the IRA but detest their actions. Approve of a United Ireland, but not at any price.

"Do you feel PLO operations are a necessary stage in the road to a Palestinian state?"

"You're talking as if the *intifada* had not taken Palestinian lives."

"Some by Palestinian hands."

"Yes. I agree. But the occupation has put us in a situation where violence has become mandatory."

Our points of view were so close yet so different. Sitting here with this confident and positive woman, I couldn't but feel humble about being a Jew, member of a conquering nation, past victims turned occupiers. I kept trying to conjure up pictures. Father forced to administer to the sick in the camp, Mother surviving by her wits, beaten, humiliated. Yet the images didn't form. Like an ancient story, they stayed in the realm of words. Mother, after all, said so little and Father had never wanted to talk.

"Were you ever beaten?" I couldn't resist asking. I needed an image to anchor my confusion.

"Luckily not. But I came close enough. Quite often. Once I had dogs sent after me." Seeing my astonished face, she added, "and a couple of times I was caught between rocks

57

and bullets." She paused and then said emphatically, "I have many Israeli friends and I don't hate. Only once did I come close to hating. There was a demonstration at the university but many students didn't go out. They were in their dorms, studying or reading. One was in the shower, one was sick and asleep. The army came in to try to catch the students who were demonstrating. They couldn't, so they went into the dorms and dragged out the students who were either asleep or in the shower, the sick and the silent. The first person we saw was a student who just came running out like a maniac. He couldn't see, he was covered in blood and his whole body was bruised. He staggered and we had to carry him in. Then we ran to the dorm and stood in front of the army and said stop it. They were dragging the students out and beating them. And these were students who were not even part of the demonstration. The soldiers looked vicious, as if all their bitterness came out on those defenceless students. They were beating them with the butts of their guns, stamping on them, in front of us. And the look on their faces made me hate those soldiers. I didn't feel sorry for them. They enjoyed inflicting pain. So much pain. And they took it out on these poor students who had done nothing and who were completely defenceless. It was really the lowest level of human behaviour."

I felt nauseated.

"The look on the faces of these soldiers was certainly one of hate," Najar continued. "They were only kids, some younger than the students they were beating. But you felt they were afraid of us. I think all Israelis are afraid of us, particularly since the *intifada* started. And this is very strange. It's strange because they have always won but they are not very sure they are winning this time round. They're afraid because the Jews have always suffered. They use this as a justification for inflicting suffering on us. And they fear that we'll use our suffering on them eventually, if we ever get to stand on our own two feet. But this is entirely illogical since we are consciously working to educate a new, healthy generation who won't have to hate."

"But surely most Palestinians do hate?"

"You forget that most Palestinians have a good reason to hate," Najar said. "I found it easy to hate the soldier who shot a five-year-old child and claimed later that the kid was trying to get his weapon, that he shot in self-defence. I went crazy when I heard it. I knew this child. He was a lovely kid." Najar's face contorted with pain. "Imagine a soldier saying he shot a five-year-old in self-defence. But if you give a soldier who is still a teenage, a weapon, if you indoctrinate him with hatred and unleash him and his friends on defenceless civilians, what's going to happen? A disaster."

I felt Najar understood the Israelis, her oppressors, better than some of them understood themselves. Having witnessed the incident the previous week, I was beginning to understand how fear directed so much of the action here.

"What really bothers me," Najar said, "is how the Israelis can internalize and take upon themselves the burden of their actions? I've seen houses sealed off, people kicked out of their houses at night, houses blown up, people deported. I've seen them breaking legs of young demonstrators, firing plastic bullets, making old men crawl on all fours and bark, humiliating women who could have been their mothers."

I shivered later that day when I reflected on Najar's last words: "If you place yourself in the position of the people you are doing this to, how can you bear the burden of your guilt? And particularly when you take into account your people's recent past?"

"Palestinian Najar Feidy," I wrote in my next dispatch, "lecturer in history, intellectual, intelligent, is confined to her house by a military governor afraid of the voice of articulate, courageous Palestinians. Confined to her house, not because of violent actions, but because of the strength she is giving her people. And because of the understandable underlying Jewish fear. Because of Israeli determination, again understandable, that Jews are never going to be victims again. Not after the Holocaust. Israeli Rachel Levy, left-wing journalist, intelligent, courageous, shares Najar Feidy's views. But, being Jewish, she is free to take part in anti-government demonstrations in the town squares, print subversive pamphlets, write articles criticising the occupation and the occupiers. Allowed to come and go as she pleases. Thanks to Israeli insistence on democracy. Again understandable.

"Two women. Two sets of rules," I wrote sharply, fast. All the while aware of the new clichés I was coining. The new shorthand to replace the previous clear-cut goodies versus baddies lingo used by my paper when covering the Israeli-Palestinian conflict.

Who am I kidding? Was Najar's five-year-old shot friend a sacrifice worth making in this futile war? Is the death of a child worth any war? Was Hanna's death worth it?

When Don phoned after I had faxed the piece, I could barely talk. His call seemed like a call from another planet. Not within the range of memory. I telephoned Mother immediately after and told her about the little boy. The feelings I was trying to suppress surfaced. "It's so intense here, Mother. Everyone is so Jewish. You've no idea."

"Are you all right?" Mother asked.

"I don't know. I only know I'm learning something I didn't know existed. Why didn't you tell me all this?"

"I don't think we knew ourselves. I told you."

"Yes. You told me. So much. And so little. I'll need a lifetime to begin to understand."

"Maybe not a lifetime. You're a clever girl."

"Oh, no, I am not, Mother. I'm only beginning to see how little I know. How much there is to know."

Mother's sigh sounded near. "Don't be afraid, Patricia. I know it must be painful, but you sound as if you've got to find out. And you have to do it for yourself. For as long as it takes."

CHAPTER THREE

I read *Women on the Edge of the Abyss* before I interviewed
Samarra Haled, novelist and public relations officer for the
Palestinian Women's Trade Union. The language, even in the
stilted English translation, was flowery, full of acrobatic
arabesques. Divorced, and the mother of two grown
daughters, Samarra belonged to the outlawed West Bank
Communist Party. She was a tall, beautiful woman in her late
forties, with deeply furrowed forehead and nervous fingers
which she kept wringing as she spoke. She was bitter against
her parents for making her marry a respectable Nablus doctor
at nineteen. Against her ex-husband for making her cook for
his large family while what she wanted to do was to
complete her university education and write novels. And
against her male colleagues.

As I sat in Samarra's Nablus book-lined apartment, I
prewrote the interview in my head. Something about women
in a war zone, who shape politics by getting out and leading
the masses.

"Women here cannot escape their fate," Samarra was
concluding the interview, slowly and deliberately, "Because
they are not educated, they cannot see an alternative to going
on to the barricades and stoning the soldiers or crying in
front of the television cameras. The trouble is that our men

do not support us properly. So we have to get organised ourselves. Because being a divorced, liberated woman, like me, means living incompletely, leading an abnormal, unhealthy life in our society. It's tough, because our men are not yet liberated."

The evening drew in and the surrounding barren hills loomed dark through Samarra's window. The interview over, she offered me a drink, but I preferred to return to Jerusalem. Samarra smiled, the first smile since I arrived some two hours earlier. "Are you afraid the Israeli soldiers will beat you?"

"What nonsense, Samarra. This is unknown territory. Travelling alone in the dark is frightening."

"If you're afraid," Samarra laughed, "why don't you stand outside the military governor's and wait for a taxi there?" There was something chilling in her laugh.

I decided to do just that. Samarra didn't see me to the main road. Standing outside the governor's Taggart Fortress, a yellowing remnant from the British Mandate days, where the road was lit, was less scary than standing by the deserted bus station. A taxi stopped and a nasal voice asked, "Going to Jerusalem, miss?" I was startled. I peeped into the taxi and saw two dark-eyed men in their twenties looking at me, smiling.

"No, thanks, I'm waiting for a friend."

The man sitting in the passenger seat opened the taxi door and started moving slowly towards me. He was short, dressed in dark grey slacks and an open-necked white shirt. A jacket and tie were thrown on the back seat: he looked like a bank clerk or a civil servant. He stood several steps away, eyeing me.

Look him straight in the eye. Don't flinch. If in doubt, engage him in intelligent conversation, I remembered the advice given by an expert on self-defence for women in the women's page of my paper. I looked at him, but his smile unnerved me.

"Come," he said, his voice soft, his accent almost British. "We're going to Jerusalem."

"No." And then more loudly, "I told you, no."

I realised I was panicking when a jeep stopped with a screech and a deep voice called my name. Before I turned to see who it was, I noticed the Arab's frozen look.

"Get into the jeep," said the driver whom I recognised as Colonel Daniel. He addressed the two men curtly, in Arabic. They mumbled something, sounding scared. He then waved them off with more angry words.

I climbed into the jeep and turned to meet Colonel Daniel's incredibly blue stare.

"I hope you found our famous novelist interesting enough to risk this," he said, pointing at the distancing taxi.

"Interesting enough. And thank you. For rescuing me."

"You're completely mad," he said, "to try to get to Jerusalem from here at this hour of the evening. Haven't you heard of the *intifada*, for God's sake?"

"Sorry, Colonel." I wasn't going to ask him how he knew I was seeing Samarra. Our previous meeting had prepared me for this.

"You'll laugh," I said when he didn't answer. "Before I left her house, she made some wisecracks about being beaten up by Israeli soldiers and advised me to stand outside the military governor's office."

"The cynical bitch," Colonel Daniel said. "Why bother?"

"I'm doing a book about Israeli and Palestinian women."

"How many Israeli women have you already interviewed?" Daniel asked mockingly. "Or are you going to specialise in oppressed, left-wing Israelis and down-trodden Palestinians who would happily see you taken to some remote wadi and raped where no one can hear you?"

Astounded by his anger, I said nothing.

"I can introduce you to some interesting Israeli women," he said. "Women whose sons died in the wars. Women whose husbands serve in these god-forsaken territories. Shoah survivors who still cry in their sleep."

I looked at his sharply defined profile as he drove along the dark road. "I might take you up on that. It's been easier to find these Palestinian women. And they have a very definite story to tell, you must admit. But I have every intention of interviewing a cross-section of Israeli women. I've only been in Israel a little more than a week."

"I know," he smiled. "Sorry. I just got angry at those bastards. So angry I didn't even take their names or ask for their identity cards."

"They were only men trying their luck. We have them in Dublin, too. Recently I covered the death of a young girl whose father raped her repeatedly since she was little. Until she killed herself."

"I'm sorry now I didn't take their identity cards," Daniel said, still angry.

"Do you ever stop working?"

"Rarely," he smiled. "In my job, it isn't easy to stop working." He paused for a moment and then asked, almost softly, "will you have dinner with me tonight?"

"I feel I shouldn't, but yes, thank you. You saved my life, didn't you?"

Daniel laughed lightly. "Why do you feel you shouldn't?"

"I don't know. It's just that I have a terrible feeling of *déjà vu*, I don't know why."

"Is it because of your affair with your editor back in Dublin?"

"This is going a bit too far." I was getting angry now. "Not only did you know I was meeting Samarra, but now that. How far back do you investigate people? Why do you need to know everything? You aren't planning on recruiting me, I hope. Because if you are, forget it."

Colonel Daniel laughed loud and long. "That was the best thing I've heard all day. You've been reading too many thrillers."

"Then why? Surely you don't investigate every journalist who comes here. Or do you? Because if you do, this will be one hell of a terrific story. My newspaper will be delighted to publish it. I can see the headline: Israeli *Shin Bet* probes into visiting journalists' private lives."

"Have no worries, Patricia," Colonel Daniel said, using my name almost cautiously. "I've been curious about you since we met with that silly boy, Avi. Was that his name?"

"I don't believe this." My rage mounted. "Do you always use secret service tactics when you're curious?"

"Not normally. But we had someone on a job in Belfast. Something to do with Libyan arms for the IRA. So I asked him to make a couple of calls for me. I hope you're not upset," he said.

"Sure, I'm upset. If this is your starting ploy, what can I expect as a follow-on?"

"To tell you the truth, I came here to meet you. I knew you were meeting Samarra Haled. She's under house arrest, so we must watch her. We know her timetable. And I suspected you might want to go to Jerusalem in the dark. As you saw, it can be pretty dangerous here for unaccompanied women."

I started to feel the fear, familiar since Alison's death.

"Listen, Colonel Daniel," I started.

But he interrupted. "Cut the 'Colonel' bit," he said. "We're not formal about ranks here. Call me Dani."

"Oh, for God's sake, Dani, what is it that you want of me?" I said, my fear rising.

"I don't really know," he said. "I suppose it has to do with being in control."

I sensed he'd confessed something he shouldn't have. "I too like to be in control, but I must admit I'm not feeling too sure right now."

"There's nothing to worry about," he said turning to look at me, his blue gaze lighting with an open smile and softening his chiselled features. "For the time being I'm only taking you to a good fish restaurant. We Jerusalemites, living so far from the sea, love our fish."

I clasped my hands on my lap and curled my toes upwards, a movement I remembered from when, as a child, I was in the twilight zone between apprehension and the need to be looked after. We continued the rest of the way saying very little. The road was dark and I didn't stop to think what would happen if a group of Palestinians should block our way as they did when I was with Avi and Uri. I asked Daniel why the streets were deserted.

"There's a curfew on," he said. "Some commemoration or other."

"Poor things," I said, almost without thinking.

"I'm sure you're trying to tease me," he said. "But you're mistaken. Many of our guys are what is called left-wingers."

When I didn't respond, he added, "Does it surprise you? As far as I'm concerned, I vote left of centre and pray for the day they'll have their Palestinian state. The day I can retire. But, until then, I have a job to do."

"Sorry, Dani. I didn't say it to annoy you. It's just that I've seen people living under curfew too often. In Northern Ireland. And it's miserable, whatever your political opinions."

"I agree," Daniel said. "It was miserable for my parents to live in the ghetto."

"Your parents were in the ghetto? Mine were in a camp."

"So you must understand," he said, very softly.

"I don't know that I understand anything. But I feel you're going to make lots of things much clearer and much more complicated."

Daniel said nothing. We were now inside East Jerusalem and approaching the Jewish part. I felt caught in a web I didn't understand. A distant memory of life with inexplicable secrets.

Daniel took me to a fish restaurant full of religious Jews where the food was homely and tasty. He suggested I choose grilled Saint Peter's fish, "straight from the Sea of Kinneret, or the Sea of Galilee, as you would have it". And he ordered dry white wine which tasted cool and clean. As he organised the meal, I kept wondering why I was here, telling myself: This is not going to end well.

Daniel was an attentive companion. He asked many questions about me, about my background and, every so often, surprised me with what he already knew.

"How come you know so much?" I asked, having told him much more than I had intended.

"Is this the journalist asking?" he queried. "Because if you're cooking a story, forget it. Stories about Israel's secret service are not too popular with the military censor."

"Censorship could be a terrific story too, you know," I retorted sharply, "just as interesting as a secret service story."

"Forget it, Patricia. You came here to interview women and write a book. And to escape that lover of yours, no?"

"Was that what your contact told you?"

"That's what you said, not in so many words," he said and I felt trapped, realising I had said too much. "So why bother with silly censorship stories? They've all been done before, you know."

"I suppose you're right." I was suddenly very tired. "I almost regret having to file stories each week. But I need the money. And I promised my paper."

"There are many stories here, not only on the West Bank, you know," Daniel said.

"I know. In this country, there's never a dull moment," I said and then smiled. "What a cliché. How many clichés. I am so tired of clichés."

"Don't use them, then. Look around and you'll find the real stories. Real people to write about. You can start with me."

"But I thought you were so secret I wasn't allowed to probe."

"You're not allowed to write, but you are allowed to probe," he smiled. The wine threw cool metallic injections into my arteries and my head swivelled. When the meal was over, I expected him to make a pass. Instead, he offered to drive me to the hotel.

"I have a long day tomorrow, must get up at dawn."

"Round up the usual suspects?" I asked mockingly, too tired to censor my words.

"I suppose so," he sighed. "You must think I'm mad, but someone has to do it. Someone must make sure foreign journalists like you can roam freely in these goddamned territories. Someone must make sure troublemakers are

70

apprehended and the *intifada* kept in check." He paused. "I can't wait for a Palestinian state. Then I can return to my thesis."

"Your thesis?"

"You're surprised, you see. Another journalistic cliché. You journalists think that all us service people are thick-headed retired cops with nothing between the ears."

"What's your thesis about?"

"It's to do with battle reaction of sons of Shoah survivors," he said slowly. "Surprised?"

"Not really, I suppose. Not after what you said about your parents," I sighed. "I wish I could find out more about my parents and what happened to them and to my sister."

On the way to the hotel I told him what I knew about Hanna. Which wasn't much, I realised every time I told it to a new acquaintance here.

Daniel listened attentively, his forehead furrowing in deep concentration. "Funny," he said finally. "I got interested in you because you seemed so fresh and yet so lost that day with Avi. But I do believe people search for each other for a reason. And find each other for a reason." I was puzzled, but we had arrived and I didn't pursue it. At the hotel entrance he kissed me lightly on the cheek. No more. Yet I felt already more committed to him than I had ever felt to Don.

Daniel didn't suggest another meeting. He didn't say he would call. But I knew.

That night I slept badly. I dreamt I was in a white taxi with Mother and Hanna and two dark men who kept smirking. The taxi was open at the back and, as it climbed up the winding Judean hills, I kept falling out on to the road. Hanna, whose eyes were an incredible light blue, pulled me back in.

The men in the front seat were smirking and talking in fast Arabic as the car climbed upwards and upwards.

The telephone woke me as the sun shone sharply on to my face.

"Patricia," Nava said at the end of the line. "Rachel has a place for you to live. Would be far cheaper than your hotel. And more interesting."

It took me some time to realise who was speaking. My head ached from sleeplessness and confusion.

"Patricia?" Nava's voice asked worriedly. "Are you all right? Did I wake you?"

"Yes, sorry, Nava. I kept dreaming about these Arabs in a white taxi. Last night I interviewed Samarra Haled and these two Arabs tried to force me into a taxi. Then this Colonel Daniel, a guy I met when I was out with the army spokesman's people, drove by and rescued me."

"Daniel?" Nava said. "You don't mean Daniel Shemi, I hope."

"I've no idea what his surname is. Anyway, what's wrong with Daniel Shemi?"

"He's in the *Shin Bet*, that's what's wrong," Nava said.

"It's the same guy."

"Oh, Pat," Nava said.

"What's wrong with him?"

"Nothing much, only that he *is* in the *Shin Bet*, as I said. Isn't that enough?"

"I suppose so. He was nice though, apart from the fact that he knew an awful lot about me already."

"I told you. Be careful, do me a favour," Nava said.

"Thanks, Nava. What did you say about a place to live?"

"Well, Rachel's lodger has moved out suddenly. So we thought you might want his room. It's a lovely apartment, in the German Colony, not far from me. Want to see it?"

"Thanks, Nava. I'm getting fed up with this hotel. I was just going to start looking."

"Excellent. I'll pick you up at lunch-time. Have you any interviews today?"

I had nothing planned. I meant to scan the *Jerusalem Post* and wander to the Israeli Government Press Office to pick up a political story. Instead I spent the rest of the morning bathing and reflecting. I called the office and informed Don's secretary that I would do a political story this week, unless anything broke. When Roisín asked if I wanted to talk to Don, I suddenly needed to hear his voice.

"Howya, love?" said his voice. "Hope you're getting me more great stories. We already have several letters supporting those Palestinian women of yours."

"Good. How're things with you?"

"You really want to know?" Don's voice assumed its intimate tone. "Bloody awful without you."

"Really?" I said playfully. Even in our last days after I announced I was leaving and refused to sleep or even talk with him, I'd felt powerless. Now, suddenly, I felt a new sense of power. "I'm glad," I said and put the phone down, laughing wildly.

I laughed and sang as I put on a pink dress, my happy dress. I ordered late breakfast and when Nava came, I hugged her impulsively.

"You all right?" Nava gave me a quizzical look.

"I feel happy for the first time since that girl died that I told you about. I'm beginning to feel at home here."

Rachel's apartment was on the fourth floor of a condominium covered with hanging washing and flowerpots. We climbed narrow stairs and reached the apartment which opened into a bright, untidy living-room. Rachel's papers were everywhere and her clothes lay strewn on every chair. In the centre of the room was a huge desk where a computer squatted, surrounded by papers and files. Rachel was away on a story and Nava showed me into a small bedroom which contained a double bed, a fitted wardrobe, a chair and a few theatre posters on the wall. I flinched at the disorder but after discussing the rent, which was low, I decided to take it.

That afternoon I checked out of the hotel, left a forwarding number and took a taxi to the apartment where I waited for Rachel to return. I made coffee and sandwiches with what was available in Rachel's large but nearly empty fridge and settled in front of the television watching a talk show in Hebrew until I fell asleep on the sofa.

The television had gone to blurred blue when I heard the door key turn. I jumped, startled by the strange surroundings. Rachel turned on the light and, seeing me, exclaimed, "Patricia. I'm so glad you moved in." It was as natural as that. Before long, I was sitting with Rachel sipping strong coffee in the small modern kitchen.

"You should come with me on some of these stories," she said. "This poor woman. Evicted from her house by the army. Didn't even know what was going on. Her son was arrested five months ago. Her husband died of a heart attack one night when the soldiers burst into the house to search for the son. The poor woman was sitting on a rock outside her house which the army was preparing to demolish. She didn't know where to turn. Her family are either in prison or away. You know, she isn't much older than me but she already has a son of fifteen. She looks more my mother's age, with lines of pain etched on to her face."

I listened as Rachel spoke. Angry, articulate, critical, she

74

spoke on and on, allowing no room for questions or clarifications. Suddenly I realised I didn't even know where Rachel had been.

When I asked, Rachel burst out laughing. "God, Patricia, I do go on, don't I? And I keep forgetting you've only been here a couple of weeks. It was in a small village not far from Nablus. They send me on these stories because of my contacts and because I speak such good Arabic. But soon they're going to kick me out. I'm too radical for them."

"I was in Nablus yesterday, interviewing Samarra Haled."

"Yes, she told me," Rachel said. "I met her at the village today. One of her union members was involved in the demonstration over the demolition. It never ends." She sighed.

"Do you ever cover anything else?"

"Not recently but, as I said, there're signs that they're planning to change my routine," Rachel said. "Still, they need me. Not many people are prepared to rough it in the territories these days. It's become too dangerous. The youngsters often don't differentiate between press and other Israelis. I'm safe because I have a foreign press badge. And because many of them know me by now. And I don't mind. I have no family, you see, no children. But some of the guys are terrified."

"Understandably?" I asked softly.

"Perhaps. So far, it's what I want. One day I'll write the definitive book about the *intifada*. But in the meantime, the *Shin Bet* are giving me a hard time, so don't be surprised if they start questioning you about me."

I smiled and told Rachel about Daniel.

"That bastard Shemi? Be careful, Patricia. He'll stop you meeting your Palestinian interviewees."

"Nonsense. There's no way he can stop me. But you must be tired and it's late."

Rachel smiled. "Sorry, I talk too much. You're quite right. I have a long day tomorrow. Have to write the piece and then move on to a nurses' meeting in Ramallah. Want to come?"

By the time we went to bed, I had been woven into another web. No one in this country seemed neutral. Everybody had a point of view. Where did that leave me?

I spent the next days putting together a story about the uneasy national unity government. I met other members of the international press corps and officials of the Israeli government press office. When it was time to file the story, I felt like an old hand. It all made very little sense, yet the logic of it all was brutal. In the evenings I returned to the flat where I met more of Rachel's friends. Cynical, harsh and of another, no less brutal, logic, they presented a pessimistic view of any chance for peace or even talks. To them there was nothing good about Israel but the Palestinians could do no wrong. When I challenged them, they averted their gazes, implying there was little point in discussing the obvious.

I found these disillusioned men and women, drably dressed in dark clothes, amazingly reminiscent of hard-core leftist groups in Dublin. The only difference was that in Dublin these people met in pubs and drank hard as they talked endlessly about British imperialism and Ireland's sycophantic sell-out. Here, on the other hand, people met in houses, sipped cups of thick coffee and smoked as they talked endlessly about Israeli imperialism. Yet there was something heroic about them. In my article I contrasted the tired pasty-faced parliamentarians with these enthusiastic tireless fighters for the rights of the Palestinians to self-determination.

76

"These men and women," I wrote, "have engaged in their fight since the sixty-seven war. They have known, since that pointless war, that conquests could not bring peace but, unlike the left within the Israeli consensus, they are not worried about what the occupation does to Israel's soul. They leave this to those they contemptuously call liberals. What worries them is the sheer injustice of perpetuating the occupation and the price the Palestinians are paying with the lives of their children."

I didn't write about what I felt was Rachel's friends' cynicism and exhaustion, or their hopelessness, resorting once more to what I knew was a convenient cliché, casting them as the goodies in my piece.

On Friday, after I faxed my article, I went with Rachel to visit her parents in Kibbutz Elon. "You can interview me and my mother for your book," Rachel said. "She's a great example of early days socialist pioneering and I'm a great example of the black sheep of this country and particularly of the kibbutz movement."

Rachel's small Fiat struggled up the hilly upper Galilee roads. It was a clear spring day and the countryside changed between patches of urban atrocities and vast hilly expanses, covered in greenery. The sky was a very light blue and the German word *Ewigkeit* – eternity – kept ringing in my mind. I had often heard Father and Mother use this word when they talked about the breathtakingly beautiful landscapes of their childhood in what I interpreted as homesickness for the land of their fathers which vomited them out.

During the three-hour drive, Rachel talked about her childhood. "We grew up worry-free, collectively brought up in children's homes, with our parents only a stone's throw away. We saw them every day, and grew up without them, without having to fight our corner in a tight family situation. But it was a false freedom. When we woke up at night and wanted comfort, the children's home was deserted. I remember many nights running barefoot to my parents' room, and banging the door with my little fists, sobbing. They discouraged it, wanted us to grow up tough and strong. They're saying now that the kibbutz system produced many distorted individuals, people with relationship difficulties. They may be right. Look at me. Every relationship is a disaster. My education succeeded. I'm a tough cookie, hard to live with, but when some jerk falls for me, I become a doormat. So they don't stay. Where is the tough political person we entered into a relationship with, they all say. In the kibbutz we were the *crème de la crème*. Israel's whipped cream kids, they call us. Only the cream turned sour. Today's young kibbutz parents, the second generation, only agree to stay if they can have their children with them in their own flats."

Rachel never paused for breath. She looked at me and continued, "The other thing that's gone is the business of no private ownership. No longer are we about the pure communism of 'from everyone according to his ability and to everyone according to his need.' Today every member has a colour television set, whether the kibbutz can afford it or not. I've even heard of people owning their own cars. My parents go mad. Who ever heard of a kibbutznik with a car, they scream in horror. They still hanker for the days when they struggled in the most inhuman conditions to built the land and the kibbutz."

I liked Rachel. She was the sort of journalist I ought to have been, I told her admiringly.

78

"Nonsense," Rachel smiled. "It's life in this country which creates journalists like me. Here you can't sit on the fence. The doomed, like me, have to struggle. We're a nation of strugglers. All Jews, but particularly all Israelis, are strugglers. We try very hard to lead a normal life, but life here is anything but normal. And I suffer. Believe me. Instead of putting my life in order, I fight injustice."

"I suppose I've also done some of that," I shrugged. "Getting into journalism and fighting crusades was a way of coping with life. Instead of trying to understand what it was to be a Jewish daughter of survivors in a Catholic country like Ireland, I reported other people's misfortunes. Through journalism I also found myself in a bad relationship. But it's too cosy a trap to get out of. It's flattering, your company is always sought after. But now that I'm here, it's getting confusing."

"Israel is a confusing country," Rachel said. "If you're honest, which many of us are not, you'll find most of your presuppositions shattered. The myth of the Jew as victim, the opposite myth of the invincible Israeli, the myth of justice, the myth of the Greater Israel – all vie with each other, but they're nothing but myths. It's almost impossible to turn Israel into clear-cut copy. Too many contradictions. Too much of what Israel is defies logic. Logically we shouldn't still be here, yet here we are, alive and kicking, more obstinate than ever. Can you explain it? I've spent the last fifteen years trying to figure it out and haven't come up with an explanation yet."

"So how am I supposed to make sense of it all?"

"It's easier for someone who isn't immersed in it," Rachel said. "The more you know about us, the less coherent the picture becomes. So do your work now, before your vision blurs."

The approach road to the kibbutz was lined with trees and the kibbutz looked like a holiday resort, with little apartments hugged by flowers and shrubs around lawns sparkling under the water sprinklers.

Rachel laughed at my admiring gaze. "You see now how difficult it was to leave this hothouse. It's not only beautiful, it's also a large loving family, all centred on you, wishing for your success and constantly discussing you. When you leave, because it has become too stifling, they still follow your progress, read your articles and watch you on television. After all, they say, she is a kibbutz daughter. You're a hot-house flower forever, wherever you go."

Rachel's parents waited for us in their one-bedroom apartment with home-made cakes and strong coffee. Dov, Rachel's father, spoke slow English, heavy with a Russian accent but her mother spoke no English at all. Yet even without words, she welcomed me warmly. Dov and Rachel didn't speak much to each other but it was obvious the old, wrinkled man was very fond of his daughter, whose opinions he abhorred.

As we walked along the flower-encrusted lawns to the room we were to share that night, everybody along the way greeted Rachel warmly.

"For a black sheep, you seem very popular."

Rachel shrugged. "These are all my brothers and sisters, you know. Every family has at least one black sheep."

Later that evening I accompanied Rachel, who exchanged her city jeans for a clean pair of light trousers and a white shirt, to the communal dining-room where a festive Friday night meal was served. We sat at long tables and I was introduced to some of Rachel's "brothers and sisters." After the meal there was a theatre show in the kibbutz cultural club.

When I said I was fascinated by the atmosphere, Rachel burst out laughing again. "You should be here when they're fighting about a failed crop or a new factory. Or when a couple who wants a year's sabbatical is refused by the kibbutz assembly. People still don't talk to each other because of rows about how much money I was entitled to from the kibbutz coffers when I left. Things are never what they seem."

The following morning we joined a group hike up the hills. We walked for several hours in breathtaking landscapes and, on our return, there was another communal meal. My view of the idyllic kibbutz was finally shattered when I interviewed Rachel's mother, with Rachel as interpreter.

"Lea Bat Dror, meaning the daughter of freedom, was born as Lea Poznansky in Warsaw," I wrote in my notebook when we returned to Jerusalem. "The daughter of an orthodox shoe merchant, she found her way to a socialist Jewish youth movement in the early thirties. When she decided to leave home and emigrate to Israel, her parents were heartbroken. Her father had planned a prosperous life for her. He was progressive enough to understand she might not agree to marry at his whim and hoped she might instead take over the business one day as he had no sons. But Lea was not interested in his bourgeois ideals. The time had come, she said repeatedly, for young Jews to break the chains of capitalism. Getting out of the *shtetl* and working the land, working with your hands instead of trading was the only way for Jews to liberate themselves from the diaspora jailhouse, she insisted.

"Lea joined a group of young Jews and, after a tortuous journey, arrived in Palestine where they founded a small agricultural community in western Galilee. Women worked side by side with men building their small community. In the evenings the women came back from the fields and cooked meals for the hungry workers. When the first children were born, it was the women who shared responsibility for them while still putting in long working hours in the fields and cowsheds.

"As rumours about Nazi expansion plans filtered through to Palestine, Lea, like many of her comrades, wanted her parents to join her in Palestine. She took a trip to Warsaw with Dov Levinski, her Russian-born lover with whom she shared a family room. Marriage was considered a bourgeois institution, unnecessary in the progressive society of the kibbutz. By now her father's fortunes had diminished somewhat but he could still afford to purchase the necessary certificates for his family to emigrate to Palestine. But she encountered a stone wall of resistance. We are Polish, her parents kept insisting. Nothing will happen to us. But what about the religious edict of returning to Zion, Lea tried. Returning to Zion is bound to happen when the Messiah comes, her father replied. But disasters are going to strike, Father, Lea pleaded.

"Nothing she or Dov could say persuaded her obstinate father. All they could save was one young sister who, like Lea, saw through her parents' bourgeois existence and decided she wanted a new life for herself amongst Jews.

"When Germany marched into Poland, Lea and her kibbutz comrades could only look on helplessly as news of their parents ceased coming. They continued to build the kibbutz, struggling for its prosperity, shielding their children from the news.

"Lea and Dov didn't marry until after the war, when news

of her parents finally reached them. Lea, who had changed her Polish name to Bat Dror to denote her flight to freedom soon after she arrived in Israel, didn't take Dov's surname when they married. Rachel was a late arrival, named after Lea's mother who perished with the rest of the family in Auschwitz.

"We are the embers of a once great fire, Lea says. We tried to establish a new form of life, an antithesis to the eternal Jewish East European darkness. But what we have achieved, almost fifty years after settling on these obstinate rocky hills, is a society which is breaking at the seams. A society whose children prefer the fleshpots of Tel Aviv and New York. We have renounced our early ideals of not employing paid labour and most of the manual workers are Arabs from the neighbouring villages. We pray for peace, because we know the Arabs, but our government refuses to talk. And the kibbutz movement is struggling to continue to exist because we are the idea which sparked off modern Israel."

I loved Rachel's parents. Israel was opening like a flower whose scent remained secret. What would have happened if Father and Mother had chosen Israel instead of reaching the shores of Ireland after the war? How different life would have been. All the secrets. All the unuttered truths.

"You're mistaken if you think there would have been no secrets about being Jewish had you lived here," Rachel said on the way back to Jerusalem. "There are many things they didn't tell us. Many myths about their past life which have entered the memory bank without being examined. In a way, you're fortunate, discovering it all only now as an adult. At least your childhood was free of all that is complicated about being a Jew."

I spent long hours writing my notes that night. Where could I have fitted into this jigsaw puzzle? I wrote as I finished transcribing the conversations with Lea and Rachel. Where could Hanna have fitted? And Mother and Father? Growing up with untold truths deprived me of a crucial part of my being. Am I a Jew at all?

Meeting Lea and Dov kindled my curiosity. Aware of the political divide, I now wanted to meet not only Rachel and Nava's left-wing friends. I also wanted to meet Lea's contemporaries. And religious women. And women settlers. And oriental women. And women who had lost their sons in the wars.

Rachel smiled when I said this. "The picture you'll get will be too complicated to make any sense," she said. "Better stick to one story. Things are complex enough as it is."

"Is this how you make your living? By interviewing only people who think like you?"

Rachel thought for a moment. "I suppose so. Come to think of it, we're all guilty of precisely this mistake. We talk only to people who think like we do, which is why there's so little dialogue in this country. But don't expect miracles," she laughed. "People are by and large very boring."

"I found your mother much less boring than some of your friends, both Israeli and Palestinian, who always sound as if they are giving a political sermon."

"I suppose you're right. But most Israelis sound that way, haven't you noticed?"

I went with Rachel on assignments, met evicted Palestinians, heard translations of their whispered stories. It all sounded so familiar. The women recited their lines with a glazed look on their faces, just like on the Falls Road. The men, less visible, were angrier. There was a sense of unreality, as if things were happening on a giant television screen. These women failed to touch me. After a number of days I was no wiser. The stories I saw unfold were no more real than what I would read in the papers.

We returned to the apartment on Thursday after a working trip to Bethlehem. As Rachel twisted the key in the lock, the door opened easily.

"The door has been opened," she said, alarmed.

"Perhaps you simply forgot to lock it this morning."

By the time I said it, we were inside. The apartment had been ransacked. The usual disorder was replaced with a terrible mess. Papers strewn all over the floor. Every shelf and drawer overturned. The bedrooms resembled a rubbish tip. Sheets were jumbled and clothes heaped on the floor. My few belongings had been thrown all over the bedroom.

"Who could have done it?"

Rachel didn't answer. "The bastards," she hissed. "Don't touch anything. I must call my solicitor before we touch anything."

She headed to the phone but it had been disconnected.

"Rachel, what have you done to deserve this?"

"Oh, do shut up, Pat," Rachel almost screamed. "Stay here till I go and phone Oded. No. Don't. God knows who may come back. Come with me."

She pulled me by the arm and headed downstairs. Across the road she said a few short and nervous sentences into the public telephone receiver and pulled me back to the apartment.

"Can you please tell me what's going on?"

"I don't know," Rachel said. "Oded is coming. He'll

make some calls on the way and perhaps he'll have some explanations. In the meantime, why don't you ring your friend Shemi?"

I didn't know whether Rachel meant it seriously. "Do you think he has something to do with this?"

"How would I know?"

Rachel didn't really mean me to ring Daniel, she said. She spoke fast and furiously but made little sense.

"It'll make a damn good story for my paper. Do you want me to write about it?"

Rachel didn't know yet. She sat nervously at the edge of her desk, looking at the mess incredulously. "I wonder what they were looking for," she said. "There's nothing for the bastards to find here."

A light knock on the door announced a tall young man in jeans. Rachel introduced him as her solicitor. The two spoke in Hebrew and every so often Rachel translated. From what she said, I gathered that the *Shin Bet* were looking for a list of the magazine's editorial board and that Limor, Rachel's friend, had been arrested, the third board member charged with membership of Hawatmeh's Popular Front. Rachel didn't understand what they were looking for in her apartment. Oded thought they were trying to frighten her.

Oded took several photographs and a statement from both of us, just in case. Rachel poured us some bitter Israeli brandy as she started putting things back in their place. I still had to file my copy for Sunday and I asked Rachel if she wanted me to write about the incident.

Oded answered instead. "Under no circumstances. Rachel has enough trouble as it is. We still don't know the whole story. Perhaps," he suggested, "you should find yourself another place, if you're worried."

I protested. I had nothing to worry about and, anyway, I wouldn't abandon Rachel now.

"It's not so much a case of abandonment," Oded said candidly. "On the contrary, you may stand in her way."

"In that case, perhaps I should leave," I said. I didn't like Oded's manner. I looked at Rachel as I said it.

"Nonsense, Oded," Rachel said. "Let her see the Service in action. As far as I'm concerned, there's nothing to hide. Everything I do, perhaps stupidly, I do publicly. You know that. And having Pat here may help to prove to them that I've nothing to hide."

"What would you like me to do?" I asked. I was getting used to feeling confused. Was anything straightforward in this place?

"You should do as you please, but as far as I'm concerne, you're welcome to stay," Rachel said. "Unless you're worried."

We spent hours straightening the apartment. Even the fridge had been searched and, as we prepared a salad for supper, Rachel kept uttering disgusted sounds about the strangers who had ransacked her flat. Later that night, exhausted but like the disciplined journalists we were, we sat down at our keyboards and wrote our respective stories. I stuck to my original plan of comparing Lea's generation's and the Palestinian women's attachment to the land. By the time we went to bed, I could hardly see. My vision and my mind were blurred. I slept badly and dreamt about Alison's dark room.

I saw Daniel as soon as I left the house to go down-town to fax my copy. He was sitting in a blue Ford Sierra outside Rachel's apartment block reading a newspaper. When I came out of the house, he lifted his head, making sure I saw him.

"Want a lift into town?" he asked, looking at me from his car window.

"No, thanks, I love walking." I tried to sound uninterested.

Daniel left his car and walked towards me. "Let me join you. I love walking too," he said.

"What do you want, Daniel?" I was irritated. "If you've come to question me, I have nothing to say."

"Question you about what?"

"About last night?"

"There's little you can tell me about last night," Daniel said. "If anything, I could tell you a thing or two. Interested?"

"Look, Daniel, I don't think I should be talking to you about Rachel," I started but he interrupted me.

"Don't worry, Patricia," he smiled. "I'm not going to ask you to inform on your friends, if that's what worries you. Can we have coffee in town together?"

I shrugged. My journalistic curiosity had been aroused. When he repeated his offer of a lift, I accepted without a word. We drove in silence to the city centre where he suggested he would wait in *Atara* coffee house while I faxed.

Daniel's clear blue eyes lit up when I approached his pavement table.

"It mustn't have been pleasant last night," Daniel started but I stopped him.

"I said I didn't wish to discuss my friends."

"Nonsense, you're as curious as hell." Daniel smiled. "Shall I tell you why your friend's apartment was ransacked?"

88

When I didn't answer, he continued, "It had very little to do with that magazine of hers. Or with her writing. Or even with her political beliefs."

"So what the hell was the reason?"

"It's all a bit complicated," Daniel said. "But funnily, it has to do with a collaborator we've been trying to pin down for a long time now."

"A collaborator? Rachel?" It was getting more confusing.

"You see, things aren't what they seem," Daniel said.

"That's what Rachel always says," I mumbled.

Daniel smiled. "She knows why she says it. Your friend Rachel is not as obvious as you think. Why do you think she's allowed the freedom to continue writing what she does?"

"You're not trying to say that she's working for you?"

Daniel smiled again. "I'm not trying to say anything. Yesterday, one of our informers gave us some intelligence concerning your friend Rachel. So someone had to check up on her. She covers her tracks well with her left-wing political activity, you see. And she has you there so no one can suspect anything else is going on." Daniel stopped and looked into my eyes.

"Won't you say anything else?"

"Not for the time being." He smiled. "I don't want to get you involved. But I thought it best to warn you to watch out for the obvious clues. Your book could be too black and white if you're not careful."

"What do you care about my book?"

"I don't. But I do care about this country and how it's portrayed. You said you hated journalistic clichés, didn't you? It's too easy to paint a simplistic picture here. If you want, I'll introduce you to some women for your book. Who would you like to start with? An oriental mother who lost a son in Israel's wars? Or an orthodox nineteen-year-old wife of a Hassidic rabbi? Or a new immigrant from Russia, arrived since Glasnost? Or a settler? Or a Shoah survivor whose nightmares take her back to the camp every night?"

I wanted to meet them all, but particularly the woman who had nightmares about the camp. Daniel looked straight into my eyes and said quietly, "You asked for it. I'll pick you up Saturday night. We'll spend the night in Dimona, a development town. On Sunday we'll continue to Ofra, a West Bank settlement. We'll end up in Jerusalem, where this woman lives. The woman you want to meet most of all."

There was no question-mark in his voice. He called for the bill and rose to leave. I found myself following him into his car. He drove silently towards Mount Scopus. He entered the university and parked the car in an underground car park. Without saying a word, he turned to me and took my face in his two hands, kissing me gently on the mouth. His kiss was softer than any kiss I had ever experienced. There was no urgency in his touch and I found myself responding slowly, without passion.

He moved away and stroked my hair. There was infinite gentleness in his touch yet I was not moved. "I'll take you back now," he said softly. "It's Friday. Lots of things to do."

I wanted to ask what he had to do on Fridays. Did he have a family, a wife for whom he had to shop at the open market? Did he live on his own and have to prepare a weekend meal? Did he go back to a mother? I didn't ask. Instead I asked how old he was.

"I was born in 1945, on the way back from the camp," he said slowly. "Conceived, I believe, in Italy, in a Displaced Persons Camp. Old enough to remember. Old enough to forget."

I wanted to ask other questions, but Daniel had started the car. I was moving in a thick fog. What had seemed clear up to now, what I had accepted without challenge from Rachel's and Abed's friends, was only the tip of a huge, treacherous iceberg.

"There's a lot I don't understand, Daniel," I started.

"I know," he said. "You're all like that when you arrive. Unfortunately, most of you leave with the same lack of understanding. Not that I would like you to simply endorse everything that is being done here. I don't myself. But I would like you to get a broader picture."

"Why?" I couldn't resist asking.

"I think it's obvious," he said without smiling. "I want you. And wanting you must mean wanting to change you, mould you so we can be together."

"You haven't stopped to wonder whether I too want you," I said, almost angrily.

"I haven't asked you for anything yet."

"Oh, yes, you have. You've asked for much more than my body. You're asking for my soul."

"I am no Mephisto." He did smile this time. "I'm not a soul-hunter. But I know a sister soul when I meet one. We are sister souls, Patricia, whether you like it or not. Whether you like the idea of a secret agent making love to you, you know as well as I do that that is what's going to happen. When the time is right."

"When will the time be right?"

"When we get to know each other better," he said. "I'm in no hurry."

"I don't understand men like you. Don't you ever consider what the women want?"

"I don't know about men like me," Daniel said. "I know

91

what I want. But I'm not going to try and get it against your will, Patricia. I've lost too many innocent souls in my life to want to lose another. Too many people I worked with died in service. Too many losses to want to lose in love too. Does it make sense?"

We were approaching the city centre and driving towards the German Colony.

"Let me off at the Khan. I think I'll sit for a while on my own before I go home. I need some time to think."

Daniel drove me to the theatre, where I ordered a Greek salad and thick black bread and read the *Jerusalem Post*. As I ate, I heard his parting words: "We'll talk again after you listen to the nightmares. Perhaps then things will start to make sense."

CHAPTER FOUR

I hated to be perplexed. I was used to being on top of things, a moulder of public opinion. In Jerusalem I was one of many foreign journalists, each believing he or she was making a difference to the way the world viewed the Middle East conflict. But the longer I stayed, the more I knew how little we influenced either side.

I sensed that Rachel was sincere. I liked her parents, liked her friends with their gauche political naivety. But Daniel's quiet certainty baffled me. And since he hid more than he revealed, I didn't know where I stood with him. My intuition was to stay away, but I was too curious.

Rachel welcomed me when I returned. "Where were you? Your paper was looking for you, someone called Don wanted to talk to you, said you could ring him reversed charge until six tonight," she said cheerfully, none of last night's anguish apparent in her behaviour.

"Screw him. If he needs to talk to me, let him call me back." I fell heavily on to Rachel's sofa.

"Bet you're tired after last night," Rachel said gently. "I thought we would do something mad tonight to cheer ourselves up. Let's go to Tel Aviv. Whenever Jerusalemites get depressed or fed up, the best they can do is go down to Tel Aviv. There are a couple of good parties tonight and we can stay the night with Yoram. Ever told you about Yoram?"

Rachel told me about her ex-boyfriend Yoram who had lost a leg in the Lebanon war, as I lay stretched on the cord sofa with my hands underneath my head, thinking about what Daniel had said. I couldn't bring myself to confront Rachel. It felt like betrayal. I would wait and things might become clearer.

"I saw Daniel today," I said tentatively.

Rachel raised her eyebrows but said nothing. "He's going to take me to meet some women for my book. Mothers who lost sons in the wars, some settlers, and a woman whom he says still has nightmares because of the camps."

Rachel still said nothing. She looked straight into my face and made me wince. "I'm so confused by this country. The more I talk to people, the more I realise how complex you all are."

"Sure we're complex. I don't know that I myself understand this society," Rachel said. "And sometimes I wonder if I haven't allowed my opinions to cloud the facts. You decide you're left-wing, anti-religious, pro-Palestinian state, and forget there are people whose sole concern is ploughing a field or producing cotton underwear for Marks and Spencer."

"Despite all your criticism, you really care about this place, don't you?"

"Of course I do. This is the only place where I can breathe freely," Rachel said. "I've tried to live in London for a while, but it didn't feel right. Every time I go abroad, I'm excited as a four-year-old, but give me a week and I can't wait to come home. I couldn't live anywhere else but this god-forsaken place."

"So why so much criticism?"

"You only criticise what you love. I suppose I'm one of this country's true lovers, although they call me Arab lover, PLO supporter and so on. I believe that freedom is never complete if it's gained at the expense of another nation, so I must keep criticising. Until things change."

Listening to her, I was certain Daniel was lying. But I couldn't bring myself to repeat what he said.

"The trouble with Israel," I said instead, "is that she has too many lovers. The love affair is too intense."

"What a marvellous headline for your next article," Rachel laughed. "Or perhaps a title for your book?"

I laughed with Rachel. "Should I go with Daniel to meet these women?"

"Do," Rachel said. "But keep your head screwed on. He'll show you an Israel I'm not able, and perhaps not willing, to show you. The Israel of victims, of Jews still living in the shadow of death."

When the phone rang I was ready for Don. He spoke a mixture of journalese and endearments, and sounded distant and false. I threw back the empty balloons of his conversation without effort, feeling numb. When he said he had phoned Mother, I got angry.

"What were you doing phoning her?"

"I just wanted to see if she was all right with you gone."

"Leave my mother alone. She knows what I'm doing and she's just fine. Do me a favour, get out of my life, will you?"

Don mumbled something apologetic and I put down the phone.

"That bastard," I said to Rachel.

"Join the club, girl," she said and we laughed until tears filled my eyes.

That night we drove to Tel Aviv where we met Rachel's friends in a crowded coffee house on Dizengoff street. Yoram was bearded and serious and I couldn't see his wooden leg although I found myself staring rudely down his jeans. The others, actors and writers, were dressed more smartly than Rachel's Jerusalem friends. They spoke of plays and books and asked me about Dublin. Later that evening we drove to the first party of the night.

I was discussing Dublin while around me people were eating and dancing. Nobody seemed to drink very much. The conversation did come around to politics but the urgency of Rachel's Jerusalem circle was missing. Here was a group of people intent on enjoying themselves, come what may. I looked for Rachel and found her deep in conversation with a young man on the veranda. As I moved towards her, a red-haired man pulled me into the centre of the room where some couples were attempting a dance. He held my waist and as the music screeched, he put his lips on my neck, keeping me very close to him, in a slow dance which was out of beat with the fast music.

I circled with him, trying not to think. When the music stopped I stepped back and looked into his face. He had a serious, open gaze and, as he stared at me, I attempted a smile. He smiled back and pulled me by the hand towards the door. I found myself following him, still without thinking. When he locked the bedroom door behind him, a swift warning flashed through my mind.

"I am Rami." These were the first words he said.

"Pat," I replied.

"We make love, yes?" he said. Without waiting for a reply, he started undressing and his body, muscular and tanned, aroused a desire I had suppressed for a number of weeks now. Since Don. Rami started stroking and undressing me at the same time. I found myself responding, my passion rising, as he kissed me demandingly. I was not used to casual sex. Don had been my only lover. Yet it was easy to respond to this direct, passionate, yet impersonal stranger. When he pulled a condom out of his jeans pocket before he took them off, I laughed, nervously.

"Why do you laugh?" He sounded hurt.

"I'm not used to this," I chuckled. "And I wouldn't know how to ask you about a condom."

Rami shrugged. "I always use," he said. "Not everybody in Israel does. They say Israel has too many problems without AIDS, so they hope it doesn't come here."

"Sounds just like holy Ireland." I laughed and my tension eased. Casual sex, never before on my agenda, was a sudden, not unpleasurable, possibility.

"You from Ireland?" Rami asked as he licked the inside of my thighs.

I mumbled a subdued yes and concentrated on my pleasure. This is fun, I was thinking as we made love slowly, passionately. I wouldn't even have to see him again.

Later that evening Rami stayed by my side, saying very little. From time to time he pressed my waist or brushed my shoulder with his lips. His touch rekindled my desire. How easy it had been, I thought, and wondered if I would manage to be alone with him again. At the second party, on a garden roof, Rami manoeuvred me into another room, where we made love, again without saying much.

At the end of the night, giddy with the warm scents of spring and filled with wonderment at my reaction to Rami's attentions, I was reluctant to return to Jerusalem, but Rami made no offers and I didn't dare suggest anything to this taciturn man about whom I knew nothing apart from the warmth of his touch.

In the car, Rachel and I exchanged giggly impressions.

"I told you Tel Aviv can be fun after all that Jerusalem seriousness," Rachel said. "I saw you with Rami. Had a good time?"

"Yes. To my amazement. I'm not used to quickies. I've been a good girl up to now, if you don't count an affair with a married man, that is. God, I know nothing about Rami, apart from his first name. I don't think he said more than twenty words the whole night. But he's a great lover."

"I know." Rachel sighed, and we burst out laughing. We were still laughing when we approached Rachel's apartment in the bright May sunrise. We slept all the following day and woke up late Saturday afternoon.

Rachel was out when Daniel called to pick me up. He stepped into the apartment, looked around and said, "New picture, this?"

"I wouldn't know. But you obviously need to tell me you've been here before."

Daniel smiled. "You never stop being a journalist, Patricia. Why don't you try to live a little?"

He was right. Since I'd arrived I hadn't let myself off the hook. Perhaps only with Rami.

"I'm right, yes?" Daniel said softly.

"Yes, I think you are. I keep thinking I've a job to do here. But I'm also here to discover the missing piece in my own life."

"And you'll go on missing it if you keep playing a part."

"I wish I knew how to stop. I could never relax. First I

had to prove to Father that I was as good as he expected me to be. Then at university, I needed to be one of the gang, and at the same time I aimed for top marks. And then I became a star reporter before I knew the basics of journalism."

"And the editor's girl, another part," Daniel said.

"I wish it had never happened. When he phones me here, I listen to his voice and wonder what attracted me in the first place. He feels so remote."

"But look at the sense of power," Daniel suggested.

I frowned. "I'm right again, yes?" Daniel smiled. "He probably became such a part of your daily life that you couldn't imagine your life without his telephone calls. You needed him to remind that you were still alive."

"How do you know?"

"I've seen such affairs many times. Had them myself," Daniel said. "In the end it's always the woman who loses out. The man may feel some pain but he copes. And when it ends, he has a home to go back to. The woman has to rebuild her life."

"Or travel four thousand miles to find herself."

"I'm glad you did." Daniel smiled. "Shall we go?"

In the car Daniel spoke about the woman we were going to meet. Michal had lost her only son in one of the ambushes set by Palestinians during the *intifada*. Daniel was involved in catching the perpetrators. This meant, he said, his voice barely rising above a whisper, sitting for hours watching the suspects' houses through field binoculars. He and his men got to know their suspects intimately, watched them eat, make love to their wives, shout at their children, prepare to go out on assignments. And all that time, Michal was grieving. She was grieving still.

It was strange, the way he talked about Michal. Daniel, I felt, was masterminding this.

"Is this woman one of your protégées?" I couldn't resist asking.

"You can say that. Don't ask me why I feel responsible. It's part of a built-in guilt feeling which never leaves me. The guilt of the survivors. It's been with me since childhood, passed on from guilty survivor parents. Michal's husband couldn't cope with Yaron's death. He went to pieces. Depression. He goes to work but says nothing all day. And her parents are no support either. They think she should have had more children and then the loss wouldn't be so painful. They're Iraqis. For them bearing just one child is unheard-of. But Michal has made her choice. She wanted to have a different life. And now she's paying for it. That makes her loss harder to bear."

We were driving south. The yellow of the sands was tinted with the orange of the setting sun. Here and there houses on the side of the wide road, squares of white surrounded with green gardens, punctuated the dusty view. Daniel had stopped speaking and I glared at the desert landscapes, fear clawing like bony fingers. Another encounter with death, so soon after Alison.

As we entered Dimona, the dark blue enveloped us, although the night was still young.

"In Ireland, it's still bright at this hour. I suppose this is one of the only things I miss, the long summer evenings. And Mother," I added as an afterthought.

"Your mother knows what you're up to," Daniel asked without really asking.

"Yes. Up to a point. I don't think she herself ever searched. She seemed to have accepted Father's decision that we should live as if Judaism was something which happened in another life, as if their past never existed."

100

"Many camp survivors forsake their religion," Daniel said.

"They never talked about it," I said. And then the rage came. I banged the dashboard with a clenched fist. "Damn it!" I shouted. "I wish they had. I wish I knew what it was all about."

Daniel stopped the car and turned to me. He stroked my hair and took my face in his hands. "You will soon," he said very softly. "You're about to find out, if I have anything to do with it."

I felt safe with my face in his hands. I wanted him to hold me but didn't have the words to ask. When the tears came, I sobbed silently and Daniel caressed my cheeks with his large tanned fingers, not saying a word. He didn't take me in his arms. I didn't have his broad body to lean on, but he was there, very still, until the tears halted. There were no thoughts as I dried my eyes. There had been no thoughts as I wept, only a cesspool of sorrow, a well of deep uncertainty.

I sniffled as I said with a forced smile, "You know, this is the first time I remember myself crying. Ever. Tears were never part of our lives." I turned to face him, swallowed hard and said, "I'm all right now. Let's go on."

Daniel, still not saying a word, turned on the engine, and the car moved smoothly on to the highway.

As Michal talked my terror subsided. Alison came to mind, another young victim of ignorance and cruelty. But paradoxically, the way Michal had worked her son's death out of her system put death in manageable perspective.

Later, I wrote in my notebook: "Why are some people so reluctant to scream their rage? Yaron was Michal's only son. The apple of her eye. Her little apartment, the proverbially

101

spotlessly clean dwelling of the humble, is full of his photographs, his sports trophies, his model aeroplanes, his beautifully precise line drawings. You could say it was a shrine, only Michal doesn't pray. Nor, amazingly, is she bitter or angry at those ignorant young Palestinians. Like Samarra, Michal is an *intifada* victim – just as Samarra is under house arrest in Ramallah, so Michal is imprisoned by her grief. All during my meeting with Michal, Moshe, her husband, sits beside her, not saying a word. When he goes to the kitchen to put on the kettle, Michal says quietly, 'Moshe has been silent since Yaron died. But I can't stay silent. I must talk about Yaron. About his death. About the senselessness of this stupid war.' Moshe comes back as she adds, 'Don't let anyone tell you the *intifada* is not a war. It's our worst war yet. Sending our kids to beat their kids. Sending their kids to throw stones at our kids. They're all children, you know,' she says. Moshe nods as if to himself. When I ask her about anger, Michal blushes. 'I don't see the point in being angry,' she says. 'I did my share of screaming, believe me. Now all that's left is sadness. And I go on *Peace Now* demonstrations, you know. Because I do believe in peace. Only peace can justify my Yaron's senseless death.'

"Michal has black, sad eyes. Her hands lie very still in her lap as she speaks, her English is hesitant and slow. She had to struggle against her own father. He didn't want her to finish high school or serve in the army. A strong-willed woman, Michal. A second-generation Israeli who defies all the stereotypes of oriental Jews who vote *Likud* and want a death to all Arabs. Tomorrow's Israel is Michal's as much as it is Lea's and Rachel's."

Daniel sat quietly all through my conversation with Michal, who looked at him from time to time, as if looking for approval. After we spoke for a few hours, Michal offered us a trayful of spicy delicacies. I ate ravenously, suddenly realising how hungry I was.

"Michal makes the best stuffed cigars in the country," Daniel said lightly as we bit into long thin pastries stuffed with pungent meat and pine nuts. As if the topic of conversation had not been death. We mopped up the hummus and aubergine salads with large pitta breads and sucked juicy black olives and pickled turnips.

I lay awake for hours after the others went to bed and listened to the sounds of the night in this strange apartment, this strange town. Why does Michal live with Yaron day in and day out, while Father and Mother chose to purge Hanna's memory? How could they avoid talking about her, thinking about her, all that time? I fell into a heavy sleep only when the pale dawn poured through the narrow shutter slits.

As as we were driving towards the West Bank, I told Daniel that I found it hard to accept that Father and Mother, unlike Michal, had never mentioned Hanna.

"They have never obliterated her from their nightmares, you can be sure of that," Daniel said. "I know. My own parents were completely undemonstrative. I never saw them hug or kiss each other. Like you, I never learnt to cry. I never even saw them fight. Only in their sleep did they scream. Mother still screams every night. Father used to moan and grind his teeth until his death. His teeth became so loose he had to have them all out. Yet they talked, almost obsessively, about there."

"Did they lose a child too?"

"Yes," Daniel said almost inaudibly. "It was only a

miracle that Mother remained alive. They took her baby to the gas chambers, but because she looked strong, they allowed her to live."

"So why were my parents so tight-lipped?"

"I don't know," Daniel said. "Perhaps they didn't believe she'd died?"

"But why didn't they make more of an effort to find her? I think they gave up too easily."

"Don't judge, Patricia," Daniel said. "We all tend to judge. I know I did. I grew up in Israel, a strong, free specimen, as they kept reminding me. So I thought they were stupid to have gone like sheep to the slaughter, as the phrase goes. Thought it was their fault, that they shouldn't have gone to the ghetto and later, that they shouldn't have gone to the camp."

He stopped talking. I looked at his carved profile and asked, "And now?"

"Now I know better. I know it was those who went resignedly to their fate who were the heroes; not us, beating up helpless Palestinians."

"Yet you do what you do."

"A paradox, I know." Daniel smiled. "It's hard to understand. It's not just what I said the other day. It has to do with having been born in a Displaced Persons Camp on the way to Palestine. With having grown up amongst real *sabras*, with always having to prove myself. And trying to be a complete contrast to what I saw as my parents' ghetto mentality. They chased me with the proverbial banana, made sure I ate enough and got plenty of exercise, and made me into their strong boy, a boy who would never have gone to the ghetto without putting up a fight. To make up for the baby they lost? Perhaps. But I'm coming to the end of the road. Almost. I've done my stint. And I'm waiting to free myself."

I found it hard to believe this was the same Daniel I'd met in the West Bank only a few weeks before.

Weren't Father and Mother brave to give their daughter over to be saved and go to the camp without protest? the inner voice asked.

As if he'd read my thoughts, Daniel said softly, "Your parents displayed remarkable courage. To let a child go so that she might be saved is the utmost act of courage. Knowing they may never see her again."

"But why didn't they say anything?"

"I don't know. But believe me, they were marked for life. Leading an alienated, taciturn life in Ireland, of all unlikely places," he said. "The rest of the puzzle you'll have to discover for yourself."

"I wish I could find Hanna. If she *is* still alive."

Daniel didn't answer.

Ariela Glass welcomed us in her Ofra home. It wasn't unlike Rachel's parents' one-bedroom house. Ariela's home was surrounded by flowers and fruit trees, but her simple living-room was full of religious ornaments I recognised from childhood visits to Marianne's house.

We sat on a low sofa, scattered with embroidered cushions. Ariela spoke with a broad New York accent and told me about her conversion to orthodox Judaism while still a university student in the States. Ariela was naive when she first came, she admitted. "I thought I would be welcomed with outstretched arms by all the Israelis and together we would fulfil the *mitzvah* of settling the land of our forefathers."

She didn't realise that her enemies were not only the Palestinians, "with whom, by the way, we lived in perfect harmony until the present revolt. I won't use the word *intifada*. Using it gives this massacre legitimacy. They don't use firearms, but potatoes with huge steel nails stuck through them, and concrete blocks, are hot weapons too. No, too many Israelis are against us. They haven't yet opened their hearts to God and to the *mitzvah* of settling his land. They demonstrate against us. Even the Palestinians don't dare write the things Israeli newspapers publish against us. But the day will come when the Israelis and the Palestinians will all understand that we shall never be moved from here."

Ariela completely discounted Arab attachment to their fields, their trees. "Give them a chance and they'll take Haifa and Jerusalem," she said adamantly. "They say so themselves. First a mini-state in Judea, Samaria and Gaza, and then the whole of Palestine. And where do we go then? Back to the gas chambers? No, the best tactic is to transfer them all across the Jordan. There are so many Arab states, but only one Jewish state in the whole world, and too few Jewish people to settle it. And if they don't want to go, we'll all live together. Even if, God forbid, the government returns Judea and Samaria as it has returned Sinai. We shall remain put on God's earth. The uprising is just another thing we have to endure, but it too will come to pass. It's tough on the men to add guard duties to their daily work. But no one complains. It's a labour of love."

Ariela left me exhausted.

Throughout the conversation, Daniel remained silent and I wondered what part he'd played in Ariela's drama. "We used the settlement as a base to trail one of the gangs," he said later. "Ariela used to make us brownies and hot chocolate and we got talking. I thought you might find her interesting for your book. You're certainly not likely to meet someone like her through your friend Rachel."

"I found her frightening," I said. "She reminds me of loyalist women in Belfast and Derry. They're sure the Messiah is on their side, and the rest of the world can go hang."

Daniel smiled. "This country is full of people who think the rest of the world can go hang. They're evenly distributed between right and left. Don't misunderstand the left, Patricia. They say that Judea and Samaria belong to the Palestinians, but they too are captives of their view of the world."

"I know. Trying to differentiate between reality and opinion doesn't make my task any easier. In this country it's hard to know where political views end and life begins."

"And while left and right battle, and people like you comment on what's going on, real Palestinian kids throw real stones and real Israeli soldiers shoot real bullets. "

"And real *Shin Betniks* have real doubts about whether their very important real work is leading to real peace?"

"You may laugh, but in this country, as you may have already found out, politics are part of life. The Greater Israel is as real to Ariela as buying bread is to my mother. And screaming her nightmares away is as real for my mother as making political speeches is to Ariela. God, I wish I could make you understand."

"What did you vote in the last elections, Daniel?" I asked.

"Talk about changing the subject." Daniel smiled. "I've always voted Labour. Does it make any difference?"

"Not really. "

"Another way of categorising me?" I didn't answer and Daniel continued, "As you get to know me, you'll see I defy categorisation. We all do. But journalists, alas, need to categorise people. Makes things easier, doesn't it?"

Daniel had shifted the argument again. So many things unsaid. We didn't talk as the car sped through the pine trees up the hilly entrance to Jerusalem. The air was hot and dry. The early afternoon sun was beating down the broad asphalt strip that was the traffic-packed dual carriageway. The heavy white heat penetrated my taut skin.

"It's going to be hot in Jerusalem today," Daniel said. "*Khamsin,* the hot wind from the desert. People are driven to madness by this wind."

He didn't tell me about the next woman I was going to meet. Daniel was tense as we climbed the dark staircase of a stone apartment house in Talbieh, an old Jerusalem suburb.

He rang the bell of a top-floor apartment and a small, light blue-eyed, grey-haired woman opened the door. She exclaimed, "Dani," and talked to him in fast, nervous Hebrew.

Daniel said in English, "Mother, this is Patricia Goldman. The Jewish journalist from Ireland I told you about. Patricia, this is my mother, Tova Sheinberg." I shook the woman's dry, arthritic hand and Tova welcomed me into her darkened apartment. "Sit, please," she said, her English surprisingly accent-free. "I'll just warm the food. One moment."

As she left the room, I turned to Daniel who was standing by the window looking out into the street, quiet at this early afternoon hour. "You didn't say you were taking me to see your mother."

"Sorry. Does it matter?"

"I wish you weren't so bloody secretive. I feel you're manipulating me all the time. Can't you ever operate without covering your tracks?"

"Old habits die hard," Daniel said, trying a smile.

"And you talk about *me* playing a part."

Daniel was about to answer when his mother walked into the living-room carrying a tray. "Please, the table is set. Dani, would you show your guest the bathroom. She would like to wash, perhaps?"

Tova's gentleness was a contrast to her son's directness.

At the lunch table, Tova's conversation was light and mundane. She chatted about London, told me about museums she had visited and theatre shows she had seen. Daniel, surprisingy lively, chipped in with anecdotes from his visits abroad. After the meal and a fragrant mint tea made with leaves from Tova's veranda herb garden, Daniel sat up, stretched and said sleepily, "I think I'll have a siesta while you and Patricia talk. She too has parents who survived the camps."

Tova nodded slowly. She motioned me towards a heavy leather armchair and followed me with a fresh cup of tea. Daniel left the room and as I set up the tape recorder, Tova asked about my parents. Which camp were they at, when did they come out, where did they go. If she was amazed at how little I knew, she didn't show it.

"We're all one large family, all of us survivors. That's why you always want to know what happened to other people. They could have been in your camp," she started. "We used to say words couldn't describe it. But over the years I've come to realise it's a mistake to think that Auschwitz was another planet, that no one can explain the horror. It was easy to think that what happened was done by monsters. Easy to forget that they were all human beings who were terrorising other human beings with the cooperation of yet other human beings."

"Does that realisation make it easier or harder?" I had started the tape rolling.

"Both," Tova said. "On the one hand, it's harder to think of it on a human scale. On the other, being able to talk about it and not just bleed internally does help."

Tova's incredibly blue eyes, so like Daniel's, and her once blond hair, saved her from the crematorium, she told me. It didn't save her baby girl who was snatched from her hands and given to another woman to carry into the Birkenau showers. "It was unusual, the others told me, for a mother of a young baby to be sentenced to life in that hell," she said. "But I looked very Germanic, despite my Polish origins, and I spoke good German. I had always been a keen linguist. Was it my luck or my misfortune to be saved, to see my daughter sent to death? The others, who had been there some time, forbade me to cry. Live, they said, don't cry."

Tova lived. Her tears dried on her frozen cheeks and then ceased completely. "I didn't cry for the two years I was in Auschwitz," she said. "Crying took away your will to live, and I knew I had to live to find Shmulik and have another child."

Tova and Shmuel Sheinberg lived in the same camp for the duration of the war and found each other as soon as the camp was liberated. "As soon as we could, we made love. I needed to have another child more than anything else," Tova said. "They now say that camp survivors had voracious sexual appetites. It isn't surprising. After all the death, we had this incredible need to live. But only those who came through. Some people came out dead. We were lucky. We survived. We still do."

I asked what made a survivor. I was really asking why Father and Mother took so many years to have another child.

110

Tova sighed. "I wish I knew. Dani has been studying this for years. Obsessed. I don't know. Some say that human beings can take any suffering providing they have a reason to live. After Rivka's death, all I wanted was to see my Shmuel again. I needed to have another child and name it after one of those who died. If it was a girl, she was going to be another Rivka. A boy was to be Daniel, my baby brother. So I hung on. Two years I hung on in that hell. And Shmuel hung on. I knew he was alive. So I lived. I stole food, I worked as little as I could get away with without taking risks, I pinched my grey cheeks to deceive the Nazis when they selected people for the crematorium, I formed friendships and alliances. And later I found that Shmuel did exactly the same. He knew I was alive. Possibly your parents also kept themselves alive like this."

It was my turn to sigh. "I wish I knew. But they said so little."

Tova turned to me and caressed my face. "It was important for us to know. To tell. For some reason it was not so for your parents. Try to understand."

Then suddenly I knew Hanna was alive.

My mind wandered as Tova talked. I'll listen to the tape later, I thought. When Tova was speaking about losing her shoes and exchanging two portions of bread for shoes taken off a corpse, I was thinking, I'll take it in another time. When Tova spoke of the liberation and of the long march to the DP Camp, where they were kept in chaotic conditions, not much better than in the concentration camp, I was thinking, I'll cope with it tomorrow.

All the time I tried to visualise younger versions of Father and Mother, in the striped camp uniform which Tova described so graphically, in stolen wooden shoes, heads shaven, faces ashen and empty of expression. But no pictures came.

"Daniel is lucky," I said to Tova. "Because you told him."

"I don't know," Tova said. "His childhood was riddled with stories. As we were looking to discover family members, as more people were arriving, broken, but determined to start a new life, poor Dani was struggling to be like the children whose parents were not survivors. As we were chasing him with food to make him strong, all he was interested in was street fights. As we were telling him about there, he was fighting to live in the here and now."

"But he knows," I said.

"Perhaps too much. His life seems to revolve around it."

"And yours too," I suggested.

"I'm afraid so," Tova said. "I've made many attempts to rid myself of the horror. I even underwent psychoanalysis to try and remember my early childhood, to bring back other dreams to replace my nightmares. All it did was make things intellectually clearer. But it didn't pluck me away from my screams."

"Do you still scream?"

"Since my husband's death five years ago, Dani says I've stopped screaming in my sleep. He stays here from time to time to make sure I'm all right. And to listen to the sounds of the night, as he puts it. I never know if it's out of worry about me or because he is collecting material for his research."

Tova laughed and I laughed, nervously, with her. "The nightmares are always the same. I see Rivka snatched away. I scream and I run after her to be stopped by this large young Nazi. He lifts his submachine-gun and aims and I stop. And she becomes a distant blur in my vision. My baby taken

112

away from me every single night." Tova paused, her blue eyes staring straight into my eyes. "I can still see her, but I don't scream any more. I start running and then I wake up," she paused again. "They tell me time is a great healer."

I said nothing and Tova continued. "Now I wake up. Usually around four or five in the morning. I've had four or five hours' sleep by then. And that's my lot. I lie awake and try to solve the problems of the world until it's time to get up. And I think about my Dani out there chasing terrorists. And I think about my Shmuel out there at his printing machines. And I think about my mama and papa and about my baby brother Daniel and wonder where they got to. And about this place. About what we are doing here and if there is a place for us. Anywhere in the world. And I try not to think about politics because if I do, I have to get up, I get too restless. What a mess we've made here. And I don't think about my Rivka. Only in my sleep."

"Do you ever think that you have formed the next generation in your own image? To remember and never forget?" I asked.

"Do I know? We've tried, but perhaps we've tried too hard. Too many people remember too much and too many people have forgotten. I don't know any more what I think about this country and the reasons for its existence. We can't go back to Poland, I know that. But who said we Jews need a land of our own? There is such a temporary feeling here. As if we've been here before and we'll go away again. Does it make sense?"

I nodded.

"You can live your whole life as a victim," Tova went on. "So many Israelis do. I, who was a victim, look around and see what we've become. Out of necessity, perhaps. Aiming our submachine-guns, rifle butts and dogs. Just because we were fortunate enough to win one or two wars. Only one generation after we were at the other end of those rifles. It isn't acceptable. Yet I go on living here, and I've never considered living anywhere else. Is that another of our paradoxes?"

It was dusk when Daniel entered the darkened room and turned on the lights, breaking the magic circle. I turned to him and winced. "Still talking?" he said, his voice strained. "How about some coffee and cake?"

Tova got up and rushed into the kitchen. Daniel put his hand on my arm. My chest ached with a pain I had never known. I placed my hand on his and we sat, silent, in the book-lined room for some moments until we heard Tova's steps in the hall. Over Turkish coffee and chocolate cake, Tova made me promise to come to see her again. I knew I would. There was so much I wanted to know, so much she could explain.

In the car I couldn't speak. Meeting Tova had shaken me. Then I noticed we weren't driving towards Rachel's apartment.

"I have a place not far from here," Daniel said. "I think we're ready to spend the night together."

It was that simple. There were no verbal invitations or sexual overtures. I did not ask if he thought we knew each other well enough. I wanted to stay with him.

We drove in silence. Daniel parked the car and I followed him up the stairs of a nondescript apartment block. The apartment was sparsely furnished. It had the air of a place a man would keep as a location for occasional assignations such as this. The living-room, dimly lit by a naked bulb, had a bare tiled floor which made it look cold and uninviting, but Daniel pulled me by the hand towards a bedroom, still saying nothing. He turned on a bedside lamp, which poured a warm weak light on a double bed, covered with a woven striped bedspread. His body cast a thick shadow on the low-ceilinged walls as he approached me very slowly. He took me in his arms and I drew close to him, trembling. We kissed slowly for what seemed like a long time. I ached for him, but Daniel took his time. He kept me waiting as he led me on to the bed and continued kissing me softly, deeply.

He started to undress me. I did not help him and when I lay completely naked, he moved back and looked at me, his incredibly blue eyes resting on my body, like a caress. Then, fully-dressed himself, he started touching me, stroking me with long motions, along my arms, legs, thighs, stomach, watching me piercingly and keeping a distance between our bodies.

My ache intensified, but I allowed Daniel's almost cold lovemaking to continue, silent. When he began to touch me with his cool lips, I felt I was opening like a winter flower. Yet the sensation of being played with, looked at, handled, kept my ache in check. Daniel's tongue touched my inside, increased my heat, but I suppressed the deep sighs my ache was sending in waves of pain and pleasure. I didn't guide his hands or his lips nor touch his body, still too distant for comfort, a remote instrument of calculated pleasure.

Eventually he undressed. Carefully folding each item of clothing as he had done mine. I lay on my back watching him and when he stood beside the bed, his body solid and brown, towering above me, I was surprised to hear myself chuckle nervously.

"What's funny?" Daniel asked.

"That I, who had been a virgin until my first lover, am now sleeping with my second circumcised man since arriving here. Fast work, isn't it?"

"Second? Who was the first?" Daniel sounded almost jealous.

"Never mind. Someone I met at a party last Friday."

"Oh," Daniel seemed dejected. "I wanted to be your first."

"Tough," I smiled. "We're back to the question of control, aren't we?"

Daniel shrugged and for a minute seemed vulnerable. He then lay on the bed beside me and took me in his arms, this time keeping me very close to him. He made love deliberately, making me come again and again, and only then thrusting into me, moaning, abandoning himself to his pleasure. As I came repeatedly, I cried and cried, my sobs smoothed by his dry kisses, his hands stroking my tangled hair and closed eyelids, his voice repeatedly calling Pat-ricia, Pat-ricia.

Much later, he brought me a cup of instant coffee in bed, and I asked him whose apartment this was.

"A friend's," he said.

"And what about you? Where do you live?"

"Ask me no questions and I promise not to lie," Daniel said.

"Another married man, I suppose. I thought we were only to make love when we got to know each other better." I sighed aloud.

"We do," he said. "I feel I know you by now."

"I don't know you. So much of you remains hidden."

Daniel said nothing. He took the coffee cup from my hand, turned me to him and started making love again.

When I woke up it was light. I was lying alone in the strange bed. The first thing I saw when I turned towards Daniel's side of the bed was a piece of paper with my name on it. "Sorry, had to go to work. You looked too peaceful to wake. There is a telephone in the living-room. Call a taxi. I've left the number and some money by the telephone. There is hot water for a shower and fresh rolls for breakfast."

At the bottom of the piece of paper he had scribbled "Thank you."

I was strangely relieved. His disappearance, I sensed, was part of a grand design which eluded me still, but like a distant tune from a dim past, my sadness ebbed and it suited me not to have to put words to the ache I'd felt so intensely last night. Despite Don, I was a sexual innocent, keeping myself like a close secret. Like the secrets life had always been filled with.

I got out of bed feeling light-headed. The living-room looked barer than last night and the tiles felt cool under my feet. There was a group of kitchen chairs in the living-room and several brown stains on the wall beside them. Naked, I moved to the kitchen and put the kettle on the gas stove. I waited for it to boil, feeling colder and colder. On a white china plate by the stove, two crisp bread rolls, a packet of pale butter and a jam jar looked appetising and I made coffee and brought it, with the rolls, back to the bedroom.

The telephone rang as I was biting into the second roll. I was not going to answer but my curiosity won. It could be Daniel, I thought as I walked towards the telephone, crouched in a corner on the bare living-room floor. A woman's voice spoke English with an Arabic accent. "Daniel there?" it said, staccato.

"He's not here. Can I give him a message?"

"Tell him Nadia is looking for him," the voice said. "It's urgent."

117

"I don't know when I'll see him."

The woman had replaced the receiver. I shrugged and got back to bed to finish breakfast. Showered and dressed, I dialled the number Daniel had left by the telephone and ordered a taxi. In the sheet of paper on which he had written the number, he had folded a note, far too large for the taxi ride. I made a mental note to give him back the change.

PART TWO

CHAPTER FIVE

Daniel

Father died in the middle of Operation Leila. Inconveniently. Like all my dead. They fall like dominoes and you have to carry on, get up in the morning and receive your orders for the day. Or give your orders for the day. And then move on to the field. And wait. And watch.

From time to time you score. Most of the time you simply wait.

When he died, they said, "Stay at home and sit *shivah*, like everyone else."

But I couldn't have let that bitch go. She was responsible for too many of my losses. Because of her I didn't get the Abu Azhar network. She managed to warn them in time. And she thought that, because she'd got involved with that young officer, we wouldn't be watching her.

Father died on Friday morning and they buried him on Friday afternoon, before *Shabbat*. He went quickly. They discovered the cancer in March, and in June he was gone. Everyone was shocked. Me, I couldn't stand the pretence.

Mother says they had to find each other after the camp, because they needed each other, needed to have another child, needed to have me. She doesn't say that what they needed was their sadomasochistic interdependence.

When I say it to my wife, she laughs. You read too much psychology, she says. Every relationship is an interdependence. People always seek out what they need in each other. We do too.

They did go on about Father. How heroic he was in the ghetto. How he was always ready to help others in the camp. God, I wish he'd known how to help his own. I couldn't cry for him. And I can't listen to Mother describe their lives as what she imagines it was.

But she knows I know. Because when he beat her at night, shouting in German, I was the only one who heard. I put my head under the pillow, but his screams penetrated the down. She was always silent. Taking the blows as if it was her due. As if the blows were the only contact they had.

All the other times they simply functioned. Lived side by side. She with her English books, correcting copybooks at night. He with his music, which she always said was giving her a hole in the head. Then he got earphones. She couldn't hear his music any longer and they retreated even further from each other. I can never remember them touching each other during the day. Or me. Never remember crying. Not even as a baby. It could be why she sent me to the kibbutz. She said it was to get some flesh on my bones. But I know she wanted to get me away from the silence. And from the screams.

Saying I had to return to the field so soon after Father's death was an excuse. I didn't want to mourn him. People said I was heartless. Going back to what they saw as my filthy work so soon after he died. I knew the tears would have to come one day. But in the meantime I had to catch Leila. My first big fish.

After her it was plain sailing. I had been there for years,

always in the field. Small-time operator. My Arabic was excellent and I knew the field, but never before did I catch anyone really big.

Leila was difficult, but getting the stuff on her and setting her up was a real scoop. Over the years, in the field and abroad, I had built up my personal network. When Jimmy phoned and told me about the maps, I leaked their existence to her and suggested, via her friend Nadia, that she should go to Ireland to pick them up.

I was lucky. The stupid bitch upped and went to Dublin without trying to cover her tracks. I had Jimmy on her tail from the moment she got in. They don't check passports between London and Dublin, but Jimmy had ways of finding out. He didn't disturb her, but he never let her out of his sight. In her meetings with those young IRA guys she behaved like a Gulf princess with buckets of money. And she made promises. Libyan arms in exchange for maps and information. Playing the big lady.

I waited for her in Ben Gurion, with the police, on the Sunday after Father's death. To see her face when she saw me was worth the whole year's surveillance. We had been watching her as she got in and out of bed with that young officer, Amiram. Never could understand how she could run this passionate love affair and at the same time connive to blow us all up. Perhaps he was part of the plan. But we couldn't get anything on her. Not until the maps.

I brought Amiram to court on the day of her trail. Didn't let him know what was going on, just said I needed his help with a difficult case. He was only a boy, really, barely twenty-one. It's a new thing for their women to become entangled with our men. In the past it was only their men with our women. But their women have become liberated.

Ruthless. Women like Leila are leading now. So no one can tell them who to screw. I should know. Nadia was Leila's friend. Or so it seemed.

Poor Amiram. She looked him straight in the eye and smirked from the dock when the military judge read out the charges. There wasn't much love in that smirk and I could feel Amiram tremble in his officer's uniform. He never saw her again, he says. Not since her imprisonment. No point really. He is going out with a nice girl soldier now.

I would have liked to have been in the service before sixty-seven. The situation was so different. Sixty-seven changed the rules. In sixty-seven I was in the middle of first year. Psychology and Middle Eastern studies. Strange combination. Preparing myself for this?

I didn't know then what I wanted to do. I had thought of the Foreign Ministry, but when they approached me to join the Service, I thought it could be exciting. It had nothing to do with ideology, just a natural sequence to my regular army service. Mother didn't want me on operational duty. Used her connections and her camp history to get me into Army Intelligence.

It's strange to be a son of survivors in the Service. A reversal of roles. The line between aggressor and victim is terribly thin. Father acted out his aggression night after night and Mother fought her pain with strength, but without tears. And I joined the Service and stood on the other side.

On the face of it, they took me into Intelligence because of my Arabic and my English. But I knew this was my way of avoiding active service, of avoiding giving vent to my terrible aggression. I was afraid of combat duty, so during my regular service I wasn't much more than a pen-pusher. No fieldwork. When they asked me to join the

Service, I thought in terms of another office job. A thinking job. I didn't realise how much fieldwork would be involved.

To my surprise, I liked it from the start. It gave me something I never had. A sense of power. And it legitimised my pent-up aggression. I'm not afraid to admit it. After Leila they promoted me. But I still spend most of my time in the field. You get to know them this way. And specialising in women, as I have done for the last while, makes me something of an oddity.

The guys laugh. Women, they say, is all he knows about. In and out of work. As if they don't all do it. It's the nature of the job. I know no officer in the Service who doesn't have women on the side. Continuously. We're all married. Most of us have children. But the habit of scheming and planning becomes second nature. I know my wife knows, but she says nothing. She never says anything when I spend a night away from home. Sometimes I wish she'd make a scene. Shout and cry like other wives. Show she cares.

But she never cries. She lives in a world of her own. Behind a thick glass wall into which I have no access. So I specialise in women, and she paints her pictures. She says she feels nothing, and she lives inside her studio glass walls.

Sometimes I think she's depressed. She's so quiet. When she went for therapy at the Women's Therapy Centre I was afraid they would tell her she shouldn't put up with a philandering husband. Thought I was her problem. When I confronted her, she laughed. Why do you think you're the centre of my world? Anyway, I couldn't change you. Everyone can only change themselves and my therapy is about changing me. Not you.

What she wanted to change she never said. But after the

therapy, she was a bit less gloomy. Although she still says she remembers nothing, still lives behind her walls. It pains me, because she is the only person I can share my world with. I wish I could share hers too.

When she persuaded Mother to go to the Centre, I had my doubts. Mother had always been obsessed with the camp. Talked about it incessantly. Father didn't let her forget. But she never cried. And perhaps she needed it.

"You need two to tango," she says. "Your mother could have left your father, or put up a fight, or called the police if she didn't want him to treat her like that. You never know, this may have been the only way they could climax sexually."

I think suffering this violence was the only place Mother could express her fears, grieve her dead. The only place she could feel anything at all.

My wife thought therapy could evoke other memories, childhood memories, so that Mother wouldn't always to always think of the camp, awake or asleep. I hoped therapy would teach her to cry.

I asked her did her own therapy bring back childhood memories. She shrugged and smiled sadly. She is a deep lake, her water as still as a mirror. But when I throw my angry pebbles into her stillness, no circles form.

When Father died, Mother stopped screaming in her sleep. My wife says that since his death, she hasn't had the need to play the victim. So there's no need to scream in her sleep. But she still lies awake half the night. And she hasn't learnt to cry. I visit her several times a week, keeping an eye. For as long as I can remember, I have been keeping an eye on her. My mother's keeper.

Mother never talks about her childhood. Says she

remembers nothing. Neither does my wife. And my childhood is nothing to speak of. We are people without childhoods. Our past is in the DNA of this country's folk memory. Concentration camps, Displaced Persons camps, transit camps in Israel, the difficult years of rationing and black marketeering. And then the present. The wars. Catching suspects. What am I saying? She doesn't catch suspects. Neither does Mother. Nor do they spend their days ensnaring. It's only I who am prisoner of this compulsion. It's true I want to get out of the Service and return to my thesis. Or partially true. Like Mother, I have an obsession with the Shoah, but I also have an obsession with cleaning things up in the field. Before there is peace, there must be security. We must know where we stand. There's no doubt in my mind that we're not the only claimants to this cursed land.

My women say it's a paradox. She never speaks of my work, never asks questions. But the others keep asking questions. How can you want complete security and at the same time believe the Palestinians have a right to their own state? Most of them don't know how paradoxical it really is. They don't really know what I do all day. From time to time I let slip things about surveillance or interrogation. Gently. Deliberately. To give them a sense of reality and get them to stop fantasising. What they don't see, and perhaps I cannot explain, is that the paradox is part of life here. Some, like Ariela, believe in our divine right to this land. But they too know that unless we murder or transfer all the Palestinians, they simply won't go away. Most of us, I believe, want to see an end to all this.

I don't believe we can win this war the way we're going. I know how much they hate us, there's no going back. The only way to get out of this deadlock is to bring it to a head. Another war will not necessarily end in our victory. Although I wouldn't admit this to Patricia, for instance. But another war will make things clearer. One way or another.

When I'm with Nadia, it's even more confusing. Finding her and making her fall in love with me was the easy part. Keeping her out of danger from her own people is much more difficult. Sometimes she stays in the apartment, but this has become too dangerous. I have found her a new place now. Perhaps she'll be safer there. Now that they know.

Sometimes my wife smiles in her quiet way and says I've brought the confusion on my own head. She never asks, but I tell her when things get too much for me. She has this blank expression when she listens, and talks about choices. "It's your own choice to live your life the way you do," she says, "and knowing you have made these choices must give you strength to continue."

I don't know where she gets her strength from. Or her amazing acceptance. I wish she'd open herself to me. For years I've been living by her side, watching her beautiful, serene features, and loving her. And all this time she has kept her distance. I ask her what she finds in me. Why she stays. But she only laughs softly and says I'm her only family, her lifeline. I ask more questions but she says, "You ask too many questions," and smoothes away my worry lines, as she calls them.

The one thing I couldn't understand when we met was her decision not to have children. I tried to fight her. "You've lost everything, don't you want to create another life?" I would plead. But she wouldn't budge. When we married she had herself sterilised. "If you want," she said, only half-jokingly, "you can have a child with another woman."

128

But in all my philandering, I never have. There must be a barrenness there, I have never taken care.

Mother says the sexual urge was strong amongst camp survivors. That as soon as they were liberated, people were fornicating like rabbits. But most don't have more than one child, at most two. Poor Mother. Their line ends with me. At times she is angry with us. But most of the time she is simply sad.

It's too late to have children now. Even if she could reverse the operation, She is five years older than me, way past child-bearing age. And so we go on, she behind her glass wall and I in the field, plotting.

One day, when all this is over, I'll go back to my thesis, researching children of survivors and how they function in battle. Preliminary studies suggest that they suffer much more frequently from battle shock. That their guilt feelings are stronger. That they can't cope with the loss of comrades. The guilt of the survivors lives on. Does my guilt at being alive dictate my choices? I look at Mother and I think, we are the lucky ones. And then I think, what's the point of being alive?

Getting Leila after Dublin, complete with maps and address books full of IRA contacts, led, circuitously, I admit, to catching that silly Irish girl who was carrying explosives for her Syrian boyfriend. Someone in the network squealed. The rest was easy. Since then we have developed good contacts with the Irish. When I got the lists from Ben Gurion and saw this Irish woman journalist was coming, I made a point of tracing her. The fact that she was Jewish narrowed the chances that she had anything to do with the network. But you never know.

And then she came out with that story about her sister.

Chapter Six

Naomi addressed the whole group. "The work is not going to be easy. We are all here, second generation to the Shoah, because we want to clarify clouded issues in our lives and this is not an easy thing to do."

Naomi's English was heavily accented. There were going to be bridges to cross, translations to make, things to explain before I could get down to working on clarifying clouded issues. God, what euphemisms. I hate euphemisms. I felt aggressive towards this middle-aged, overweight woman dressed in tight joggers and T-shirt.

Naomi looked around the room and asked us to introduce ourselves. Say our names, where we came from, talk about our parents, say why we were here, what we were hoping to achieve.

I tried to mask a yawn, but Naomi said, "No need to hide. If you're tired, or bored, or angry, this is the place to express it." I felt waves of anger flooding my tired mind. But I shrugged and said nothing.

Naomi turned to me. "Why don't you start? I can see you're angry. It'll do you good to be the first to get whatever it is off your chest."

I didn't want to be the first. I said nothing. Naomi looked at me with her large, watery eyes and motherly, expressionless face. Nobody said anything. All waiting for me to start.

I heard my voice as if coming from a distance. "My name is Patricia Goldman." I paused.

"You're very welcome, Patricia," Naomi said. "Would you like to tell us about yourself? Where you're from, that sort of thing."

"I like to be called Pat. Or Patricia," I said very softly. And then, dismayed, I added, quickly, "I don't know why I said that. You wouldn't know what else to call me."

"Was there someone who called you something you didn't like to be called?" Naomi asked.

"Yes, but it doesn't matter. I come from Ireland. Dublin. And I feel I'll have to do a lot of explaining in this group."

"We're all different," Naomi said. "But also similar. All of us have survivors for parents. I know how you feel, Patricia. Give it some time. It can only get easier. Would you like to tell us some more? Why you're so angry, for example?"

"Oh, I'm not really angry. Just confused. And tired," I said. "And scared."

"What are you scared of?"

"Secrets," I whispered.

And then I talked. About my family secret. About finding out. About feeling that there were more secrets buried deep in the family history. And about how little I knew about these secrets, about my parents' past. About Don and about coming here and landing in another, more complicated, less suitable relationship. About running away.

I spoke fast and softly, looking down all the time and from time to time passing my hand through my hair, exorcising dark shadows.

132

When I paused for breath, Naomi spoke. "There is a lot to work on here," she said, but now she wanted the other group members to introduce themselves. She looked straight into my face, smiling, nodding.

I heard the other women tell their stories as if in a daze. Not really listening. By the time Alice, a tall Californian, was talking about how her mother married her father after the camp, when they were both alone in the world, hurriedly, without love, just to make contact with another human being, I felt suddenly nauseated. I didn't want to have to deal with all their stuff, I thought. I needed help. Now. I didn't want to wait until we all had our turn.

Naomi seemed to sense my doubts. "I can see you're still angry, Patricia." She turned to me. "In order to be able to proceed with our work, which is mutual therapy, it is best to clear this anger before it becomes a problem. Would you like to tell us about it?"

I felt strangled. I couldn't speak. But Naomi was staring at me and the group waited quietly. "Oh, it's just that I didn't think it would be like this," I blurted out, indistinctly. "I came to the centre for help. For me. I'm a journalist, well used to listening to other people's stories."

"And now you want our undivided attention, is that it?" Naomi's kind voice enquired.

"I suppose so," I whispered.

"But listening to others is part of the therapy," she said. "You may find you're not alone, after all."

I felt trapped once again. Finding myself in the Jerusalem Women's Therapy Centre had been, as were lots of things now, Daniel's idea. It had helped many women he knew, including his mother.

The summer had come quickly and Jerusalem, dry sandy-coloured stones enclosing endless human commotions, felt like a boiling pot, ready to explode. I spent a lot of my time with the international press corps, trailing from briefing to press conference, from eviction to demonstration, from government crisis to *intifada* incidents, from gunfire to the stench of burning rubber. Life with the pack had its compensations. I got to know all the famous names I had met on the television screen, old war zone hands, experts in the art of sifting for informational gems in the oceans of words. My work was facilitated by experienced hacks who knew where the real stories lay. It seemed that all I had to do was follow.

Most of them were cynics. They had seen it all, lived through it all, and there were only a few things which could still shock or surprise them. Gradually, with the pack on the one hand and Rachel and Daniel on the other, I too developed a certain cynicism. It wasn't unlike being back home, covering political crises and IRA attacks, translating it all into column inches and usable copy. After two months, I began to feel my copy lacked the early urgency, or originality. In his telephone calls, less frequent now, Don urged me to dig harder for stories. I was beginning to sound like one of those hacks, he said, his tone harsh. Couldn't I find some blood-and-guts stories?

From time to time things did move me. Like the journey with Rachel's friend Ora to visit her son at his initial training camp, somewhere in the West Bank. "We were sitting in Ora's battered Renault," I wrote, "and the boys who were stoning us were the same age, the same size, as her eleven-year-old son, Yonatan. Yonatan sat by his mother, his eyes wide open and his little face blank. Ora drove without looking to either side, determined to get us there in one piece. None of us spoke. Ora cursed in Israeli Arabic (the Israelis favour Arabic for curses), softly, under her breath. When the camp came into sight, she stopped the car and burst out in bitter tears. 'What have we done to our boys?' she sobbed. 'How can they cope with these little boys, not bigger than their little brothers? How can they fight them with guns and remain our kind, honest, pure-hearted boys?'

"There was no consoling her. I looked at her and at Yonatan. He didn't cry, but he took his mother's head in his hands and stroked her greying brown hair without speaking. When a war between two warring nations is translated into this, all you want to do is shake Messrs Shamir and Arafat and ask them, is this what you dream of when you think of your respective Jewish and Palestinian states?"

But, on the whole, I had to admit that Don was right. My copy was getting softer, as the picture was becoming more complex. And the time was coming when I'd have to make up my mind about returning to Dublin. My three months were almost up as the sun beat relentlessly high in the late July skies. Every week Don reminded me that they were expecting me back in the office soon.

Daniel, meanwhile, was fading in and out of my life irregularly, but always appropriately, as if sensing what it was I was thinking of. He found me late one night after I had ventured on my own to a foreign correspondents' party at the American Colony. He was waiting outside the hotel in his car as I stepped out to look for a taxi. He chauffeured me without speaking to the flat and made love to me, intensely, staring at me as I cried my pleasure.

He materialised in Rachel's apartment when I was alone for four days and Rachel had gone to Egypt with a friend. We spent three nights in my narrow bed, with Daniel

135

disappearing in the early hours of the morning, leaving me bleary-eyed and grey with tiredness, my heart heavy with an unfamiliar mixture of vivid happiness and terror.

He never telephoned, but he always knew where I was going to be. When I questioned his methods or their morality, he laughed. He was well used to finding people when he needed to, he would say. Once or twice I saw him at a restaurant. Always late at night. Always alone. He would come to my table, greet the people I was with, all of whom he seemed to know, and move on, wandering, taking a drink at the bar or joining friends at another table.

My life assumed a set pattern. By day I rode with the pack, or met women for the book. At night Rachel and I went out to the YMCA, Fink's, The Hut, Gilly's, where media people and people of similar political persuasion to Rachel were hanging out.

Rachel became a close friend. I could talk to her about my articles, about the people I met, about plans for the material I was accumulating. About everything but Daniel. Rachel would not be drawn about him. She did tell me he was married, as I had suspected, but said very little about him or his wife. When I suggested she knew more than she was saying, she would shrug and say nothing.

By the end of July I hadn't got much closer to understanding. I glided by the conflict using well-worn shorthand phrases to describe the contenders. I was still on the outside looking in.

I met Rachel's friends and there were long discussions well into the night about the wrongs of the occupation. I joined the *Women in Black* peace vigils on Friday afternoons and together with them was abused by passers-by. I retreated afterwards to one of their regular coffee houses in the German Colony, to plan the next move with them. I covered the work of the Civil Rights League, watchdogging human rights infringements. I attended *Peace Now* demonstrations, listened to Amos Oz and other well-known, internationally translated Israeli authors talk about the corruption of Israel's soul. I saw theatre shows in Arabic in East Jerusalem, fantastic realism depicting Palestinian oppression, creatively, with humour. I met more Palestinian women, all highly educated, highly articulate.

And still I remained on the outside.

When I complained to Daniel, he laughed and asked if I expected to be allowed in after nine weeks in the country. I was frustrated. Not just because my writing was becoming predictable, but because of my growing desire to belong.

One night, when I was returning from town having left Rachel with friends, Daniel was standing outside Rachel's apartment block. As his light blue eyes smiled, my stomach contracted.

"There is someone I want you to meet," he said with no introductions. "She would be great for your book."

I was tired. "Not now, Dani. Why do you always wait for me in the dark?"

Daniel took me in his arms and kissed my mouth softly, barely touching my lips, holding me very close to his large body. "What's the matter?" he whispered. "I come to see you when I can. You know that."

I shook myself away from his tight hold. "I don't understand you. So many things I don't understand."

"Let's go to the flat," Daniel said. "We can talk."

"I'm tired." Suddenly I didn't see the point.

"Just for a short while," Daniel said. He pulled me gently

137

towards the car. What am I but a follower of men, I thought as we drove silently towards the flat. Always dancing to their tune.

When we got to the flat I was ready to explode, but Daniel muffled my anger with kisses.

When we lay, spent, between the damp sheets, Daniel told me of the woman he wanted me to meet.

"She's a Palestinian moderate. Someone who's prepared to talk to us without the PLO umbrella. There are more like her than the media or the politicians of the left would admit," Daniel said.

"And why would she talk to me?"

"Precisely because she believes it's important to present the moderate point of view. They, the moderates, believe they're the future of the territories. They don't believe a Palestinian state on the West Bank is a viable economic proposition and object to both the occupation and the PLO."

"And her personal story?"

"You'll see for yourself," Daniel said.

"Unusual for you not to want to fill me in. What's your connection with her?"

"Nadia and I are acquaintances," he smiled.

"Nadia?" I remembered. "I've heard the name before. Yes, after our first night here she phoned you and said it was urgent you called her. But I didn't see you for a fortnight, so I couldn't pass on the message."

"Yes, she told me she phoned here." Daniel smiled again.

"What are you hiding, Dani?" My rage was returning. "What is it about you? Why do I always have a feeling that you're an arch-manipulator?"

"Must be your journalistic imagination," Daniel said. "You'll find there's much less to me than meets the eye."

"You tell me nothing about your life, apart from

fragments you want me to know, about your past, and your parents. And even there I feel there are great gaps. You always know where I am but I never know where you are. At least with Don I knew I'd see him every day, even if by the end of each night he sneaked out of my bed to go back to his wife."

"I give you what I can," Daniel said. "It isn't much, I admit, but I don't make false promises." His eyes rested on my face lightly then moved to look at some distant point in the room. "I care about you, Patricia," he said slowly.

"God, why do I always find men who have peculiar ways of showing they care?" I said. "Look at me. Young. Not bad-looking. Bright, or so they tell me. Good job. I earn quite a lot of money. I'm independent in everything but men."

Daniel said nothing. He pulled me towards him but I moved away. "Damn you, Daniel Shemi." I gathered my clothes and began to dress slowly, deliberately. "I've been there before."

In the car, Daniel said he had heard what I had said, but there wasn't much he could do.

I turned to walk into the house, choked. I entered the apartment barely noticing Rachel following me into my room.

"I feel so stuck, Rachel," I whispered.

"Shemi?" Rachel asked.

I nodded. "I'm behaving like a teenager. Why am I such a fool?"

"I told you to take care," Rachel said. Daniel, she said, her voice low, went to secondary school at her kibbutz. Rachel's parents were appointed as his adoptive family and Rachel, five years younger, was his closest friend.

139

"He was a manipulator even then," Rachel said. "Too used to keeping secrets. Things weren't as they seemed at home. He never told me quite what was going on, but he had to be sent away. Keeping family secrets is never easy, you know. He was forever lying, playing one adult against another. But I loved him. He knew everything there was to know. And he played on all my weaknesses, knew all my problems, used members of my age group against one another. I was his captive." Before he went to the army, they became lovers. Kibbutz morals were laxer than urban ethics and nobody frowned, although Rachel was just thirteen.

Rachel stopped talking and I looked at her briefly. "Now I know how wrong it was. I was still a child. Today they'd call it child abuse. Then I didn't see it that way. My parents said nothing. The famous kibbutz liberalism, you know." She lowered her eyes. "I know I should have told you before. Particularly because of that girl who died. But I couldn't. You seemed so absorbed. And I thought, what the hell, she's an adult, she knows what she's doing."

"When it was time to go to the army," Rachel continued, "he didn't choose to join the kibbutz group in a new kibbutz settlement in the Negev. Instead he joined the intelligence and then the *Shin Bet*. At least in the Service all his machinations are legitimate. He hurt me, but I didn't know it then. I loved him. I got over it long ago. But I can't bear to see him hurt you now."

"What does he want from me?" I said.

"He may be getting back at me. He's never quite worked me out of his system. He never lets go, you know. What do you think was the reason for searching my flat that time? He still keeps tabs on me, reminding me of his existence in the nastiest ways."

"He said you were involved with some collaborators, suggested you were helping the Service."

"Shit!" Rachel was angry. "Why didn't you tell me?"

"I didn't know whether to believe him and I didn't want to insult you. God, how confusing."

"There's actually nothing very confusing about Daniel Shemi," Rachel said severely. "He was brought up to manipulate one parent against another. He simply can't tell the truth, though, surprisingly, he does know right from wrong. He had to justify that pointless search so he invented some story about me being an informer. He does that to me from time to time. Every time, I complain to the police through my solicitor, and every time the complaint is investigated with no result. And they never find anything in the apartment. Nor do they ever charge me."

"Do you know his mother?"

Rachel nodded. "She says she too can't understand his compulsive dishonesty. But she doesn't admit her part in his behaviour. Perhaps she isn't aware of it. I like Tova. I liked Shmulik too. But something was wrong. I don't blame them. Look at your own parents. What they didn't tell you brought you halfway across the world. There are too many secrets in that Pandora's box, that code word, Shoah. And we here are expected to take it all on board, discharge it as our official everlasting anti-Shoah anger, and get on with our murderous lives."

"Should I stop seeing him?" I asked feebly. " I never know where he is, but he always knows what I do, who I meet. Even Don was better, damn it."

"How can I tell you what to do? But if you're hoping things will change, forget it. That's the way he conducts his life. A delicate balance between his wife and his many

141

relationships, his job, his mother, his past, his present. How he has got away with it so far, I'll never know."

"He said he cares for me. What a joke."

"Perhaps not." Rachel shrugged. "His need for love is insatiable. All these affairs. He says he needs them to feel he's still wanted. To feel he's still alive, is more like it."

Nadia waited at the flat. A dark-haired, heavy-featured woman, dressed in expensive-looking yet glitzy black separates, her face heavily made up and her hennaed hair carefully combed down her shoulders. There was an over-ripeness about her. She obviously came from a world very different to mine.

"Nice to meet you." She shook my hand with well-manicured, red, long-nailed limp fingers. "Can I offer you coffee?"

It was strange being offered hospitality in the flat where I had experienced such intense intimacy. Nadia was obviously very much at home here. Much more so than me. We sat down in the living-room corner, on the wooden chairs, beside the stained wall.

"I believe you're writing a book about Palestinian women," Nadia started, polite, tentative.

"Palestinian and Israeli women," I said.

"Well, I want you to know there are other women as well as those *intifada* leaders." Nadia enunciated her words slowly, carefully. "Many of us are tired of the image of Palestinian women as fighters and rabble-rousers."

"But surely you must be proud of your sisters. They're so strong and tenacious in the face of what must be an exhausting war of attrition."

"These are empty words, I'm afraid," Nadia said. "Just

words. The lives of women are not led on the barricades, you know. There are life tasks to perform, washing to hang, meals to cook, husbands and children to look after. And there's also shopping, clothes, make-up, you know, the pleasures of life. I'm tired of the prospect of living under occupation forever, but the idea of a Palestinian state fills me with horror."

"Why?"

"A Palestinian state could not survive economically," Nadia said. "And in the end that's what it's about, don't you agree? And who will govern such a state? The PLO is not acceptable to all of us here, despite what they say. Why are they so afraid of elections? If they represent most West Bank Palestinians, what's to fear?"

"Surely your views are not those of the majority?" My curiosity about this urbane, sophisticated woman was growing.

"I'm not so sure," Nadia said slowly, tossing her thick hair with an upwards head movement. "We haven't counted, but people like me represent a large body of moderates."

"Tell me about yourself," I asked. "Why, for instance, are we meeting here and not in your own home?"

Seemingly unruffled, Nadia explained she thought it would be more convenient for me to meet her locally. And since Daniel Shemi, who she believed I knew, suggested this flat, she thought it was a good idea.

Nadia was the daughter of a West Bank industrialist. She was in her mid-twenties, but she wasn't married, she said.

"Unusual in Arab society, don't you agree?" I interrupted.

"Not so unusual these days," Nadia said, choosing her words very carefully. "Things are changing here too, you know. I studied in Paris. My father thought I would get a

143

better education there. I'm back only a little over than a year and frankly, I haven't yet met the man with whom I would like to share my life."

"But your parents? Don't they want to see you settled?"

"Of course they do. Don't yours?" she smiled charmingly. "But they have to accept the situation. I don't live at home, so they can't put too much pressure on."

Nadia was working in an antique shop but business, since the *intifada* began, was slow.

"So what do you do with your time?"

"Meet friends, talk, the usual," Nadia said.

"Why did you want to meet me, Nadia?" I said. "Because I have the feeling you're not telling me everything."

Nadia tossed her hair and looked beyond me at the stained wall. "You may be right," she said softly and I had the impression something was breaking in the brittle exterior. "I'm not telling you everything. It isn't easy to be so isolated."

"Isolated? But I thought you were part of a large majority of moderates?"

"Oh, that. Of course we are. None of you journalists have realised what the real feelings of the local Palestinians are."

I was losing her again. "Most of us have as little time for Mr Arafat as we have for Mr Shamir. While these two play politics, people in these territories are desperately trying to keep themselves alive, put bread on the table, have a semblance of social life, do business, you know."

"You said you were isolated?"

I could see she was weighing the pros and cons of answering my question. She frowned, looked down and apparently decided to speak her mind.

"I'm out of place here since I came back. My parents

always had Jewish friends, even before forty-eight. After sixty-seven they renewed their contacts and as a child I always met Israelis. I believe we can live in harmony with the Israelis. Perhaps not with this government, but Israelis as a whole, yes, definitely. And then comes the *intifada*. I came back from Paris, to what I thought would continue to be my sophisticated neighbourhood, Shuafat, to find everything had changed beyond recognition. We're afraid to voice our opinion. Jews don't come to see us any more, and we don't visit them. If you're not on the barricades, you're alienated from mainstream Palestinian society these days. Arab men are still traditional and my school-friends are either married with a couple of children or involved in this damned *intifada*. Where do I fit in? I'm scared. If we continue socialising with the Israelis, we can be labelled collaborators. And if you socialise with Palestinians, you have to be careful not to speak your mind."

"Why don't you start a political organisation for people who think like you?" I asked.

"And find my body in the gutter the following morning? No, thanks," Nadia said bitterly. "You see," she added, "things are never as simple as they look, are they? Only journalists can come here and make simple equations."

"Funny that," I said. "Everyone I meet says journalists aren't any good at understanding what's going on. But if all of you, from extreme Israeli right to extreme Palestinian left, feel that we're doing such a bad job, why talk to us at all?"

"Talking to strangers with the prospect of having our opinions printed somewhere outside this madhouse, even distorted, is a comforting thought," Nadia said. "Otherwise you feel completely isolated."

By the time we had talked for several hours, I was

145

warming to this intense woman. Feeling at ease, I asked if it was she who had rung Daniel.

Nadia was surprised. "So it was you who answered the phone that day?" she asked. "What were you doing here?"

"Sleeping with Daniel, what else?" I said unthinkingly but Nadia looked shocked. "I'm sorry, I shouldn't have been so direct."

"Never mind," Nadia said softly.

"You too? Oh, dear," I said when Nadia didn't reply. "How embarrassing. So this is why you know this flat so well."

Nadia still said nothing. I fiddled with the tape recorder, trying to avoid looking directly at Nadia's face.

"This is another reason I feel so isolated," Nadia whispered. "But I don't want you to put this into your book."

"Of course." I turned the recorder off and put it down beside my chair. "You must find it difficult having an affair with a *Shin Betnik*."

"He told me about you and said I should meet you. He never mentioned that you and he . . ."

"Were sleeping together? Because that's all it is, Nadia. I'm only here a couple of months and we sleep together from time to time. No need to feel jealous."

"With Daniel it's never simple," Nadia said sadly and I thought, how right she was.

"I suppose I knew I wasn't the only one," Nadia added.

We started laughing, nervously, but Nadia was visibly hurt.

"This is why it seemed I wasn't telling you the whole truth," Nadia explained. "I suppose I am ashamed of this liaison. I have to keep it hidden from my family, although I have the feeling they know. And watch my every move."

146

"What will you do?"

"I don't know. I might go back to Paris. There isn't much of a future for me here. Palestinian men are either too traditional or too involved in the *intifada*. And Jews are out of bounds."

"And life without a man isn't an option, I suppose. Couldn't you be a career woman?"

"You must be joking. In Arab society?"

"I still don't understand, Nadia. Why did you want to meet me?"

"Oh, I don't know. Daniel suggested it. Put across a moderate viewpoint, he said. It's a point of view the Israelis want to encourage, no?"

"Yes. Daniel the manipulator." I sighed and we laughed again.

"Do you come often to this flat?" I asked.

"Not too often now. When he can find the time. You must know how it is."

"Whose flat is it, anyway?"

"Oh, I think it belongs to the Service," Nadia said. "Haven't you seen the bloodstains on the wall? It has become too dangerous for me to be seen here. I have another place where we meet. Safer."

"What a precarious life you lead," I felt for this sad woman, mellow beyond her years, whose careful good looks were beginning to fade.

Later that night, over a cup of hot chocolate, I questioned Rachel about Nadia.

"He sent you to meet Nadia Bushari?" Rachel seemed amazed. "Did he tell you that her grandfather was killed by the PLO in the early seventies as a collaborator? And that her father has been involved in a long-drawn-out series of court cases? He was accused of bribery."

"Of course he didn't." I smiled sadly. "Nor did he say that he and Nadia were lovers."

"That explains it." Rachel was angry now. "Sending you to meet her as a representative of the moderates is one thing, but putting you in the same seat, as it were, with his collaborator mistress is quite another."

The following morning Rachel called me from the office. "Come have coffee with me in *Atara*, I have some information you might find interesting," she said cheerfully.

I had slept badly the night before, trying to puzzle Daniel's motives in involving me in his webs. I was growing to despise and fear him, yet there had been an inevitability about my attraction to him.

"I couldn't wait till this evening to tell you what I found out about Ms Bushari," Rachel said, munching a croissant energetically. "I couldn't speak on the phone, you understand. Now that you've been there, I think the flat has been bugged continuously, whatever about watching me."

She looked into my face and announced almost cheerfully, "Well, our Nadia is part of a well-known network of Palestinian informers. I wonder which came first, being recruited to the Service or getting her to fall for Mr Shemi."

"What a cynic you are, Rachel," I said.

"I suppose I've learnt to be one," Rachel agreed. "You can't survive otherwise in this town, or in my profession. When I go abroad and meet perfectly ordinary people who express affection and show enthusiasm as a matter of course, I realise how many of us have adopted the 'I criticise therefore I exist' mode of living. It's sad, I agree, but without it we would be completely taken over by the real cynics, by the Daniel Shemis of this world. My sources say he has made women his speciality. Be careful, Pat, I implore you."

That weekend, Don told me that if I didn't return on the due date, my job could not be kept for me. If I decided to stay, they would continue to buy copy from me, but not every week. "We can't afford a regular Middle East column," he said and I detected a certain glee in his voice. He would, of course, prefer it if I did return. He missed me, he added.

I wasn't ready to return. But I didn't know whether I would be able to keep myself without the paper's regular pay cheque. I called Mother. I needed to stay here longer, I told her. But I wasn't sure I could survive financially. I could hear Mother breathe deeply and slowly at the other end of the phone.

"If you have to stay, stay," she said in her measured voice. "I shall pay your mortgage until you decide what you have to do. And I can look for a tenant and send you the rent. If you have to stay, stay," she repeated.

"Are you sure, Mother? Will you have enough?" I felt as if a heavy hand had released its firm grip on my throat. "I do have to stay. I feel there's so much I need to find out."

Within twenty-four hours I had a reporting job with a minor American agency. I telephoned the editor and told him I wasn't coming back. Mike said he would have to advertise my job. "But there'll always be a place for you with us. In the meantime, send us copy when things hot up."

Firmly ensconced now in a Jerusalem I was growing to love, my tight work schedule left less time to spare for meeting Daniel. But I wasn't surprised to find him waiting after one particularly hectic night shift, three weeks after my meeting with Nadia.

149

"How's the new job?" he said, without introduction.

"Grand, thanks. Took you a while to check me out."

"I won't tell you when I did find out," Daniel smiled. "Fancy a meal?"

Over an array of pungent oriental salads and a bottle of full-bodied red wine, Daniel quizzed me gently about the new job, about my decision to stay. I answered his queries lightly, until I could take the empty chatter no longer and said sharply, "What were you playing at, Dani, sending me to meet that Palestinian collaborator?"

"Collaborators have a story to tell too. If you weren't so entrenched in your views, you would be able to see that Nadia is formidable material for your book."

"Yes, but you know that the best parts of her story aren't for publication. I could endanger her life if I told the story of a middle-class Arab woman just back from Paris, who didn't know where her loyalties lay and found herself hopelessly entangled with a manipulating *Shin Betnik*. They'd have found out who she was even if I disguised her identity, wouldn't they?"

"There are many ways of telling a story, I don't have to tell you," Daniel said calmly.

"What are you playing at?" I shouted. "She was so hurt when she found out that you and I . . ."

"You and I what?" Daniel asked, his eyes smiling mischievously.

"Well, you know." Suddenly I couldn't find the words to describe what we had, realising how much it meant to me.

"Yes," Daniel said very softly. "She had to find out sooner or later."

When Daniel put his hand on my arm, I recoiled as if his hand was red-hot. Shivering, I felt the old fear engulf me again. Like when Alison died.

150

"And what about Rachel?" I said. "The stories you told about her being a collaborator and all the while you were only keeping tabs on her because you were once involved with her? When she was a kid in the kibbutz."

Daniel stared at me. "You're beginning to catch me, Patricia. Soon there will be very little you won't know."

"Aren't you going to offer an explanation?" I said.

Daniel shrugged and smiled sadly. "Some things I can't explain. They happened. I told you, secretive habits die hard and when others are involved, it isn't always possible to tell the truth."

Later that night as we made love, I watched his face as he made me come, and saw pain behind the light blue eyes. But he said nothing and even his pleasure groans were soft, like large, woolly clouds descending on a calm ocean.

When the phone rang, he jumped from the bed like a well-trained soldier and answered in staccato Hebrew. He returned to the bedroom and started dressing fast, without a word. To my queries he said laconically, "Have to go. Emergency. You know how to get yourself home, yes?"

He slammed the door shut without waiting for a reply and I spent the night dreaming about Alison.

When I entered Rachel's apartment in the early morning, Rachel was up waiting for me in the kitchen. "Were you with Shemi last night?" were her first words.

I nodded and turned to go to the bathroom. "Wait," Rachel said and something in her voice made me turn and look at her. Her eyes were bloodshot and her hair dishevelled. "Didn't you hear?"

Nadia, Rachel told me, almost accusingly, had been brutally murdered last night. While Daniel and I were making love.

I shivered. As I stared at Rachel, my eyes filled with tears. Remembering my dream about Alison, my sobs became uncontrollable. I cried for Alison. For Nadia. For myself. Rachel, still angry, held me, cried with me.

The morning papers had details of Nadia's murder. She had been raped and stabbed several times before she was allowed to die. Her killers had shaved off her thick hair and hung placards in Hebrew, Arabic and English, "Zionist whore".

"I bet Shemi is going to hound her killers now," Rachel said bitterly. "Damn him."

"But many Palestinians are killed by their own," I said tentatively. "What do you expect? She was an informer. And she was involved sexually, all the more reason for them not to trust her. From their point of view it makes perfect sense, can't you see?"

"I don't know what makes sense any more."

I was suddenly very tired.

During the days after Nadia's death, I did my work at the agency mechanically. I was grateful not to have had to cover the murder; the night shift had covered it. I didn't send the story to my own paper. "They asked me to, after seeing the story in the English papers. But I couldn't. I feel too involved," I explained to Rachel.

I couldn't help coming across the story again and again. Fred, a veteran reporter from Edinburgh, showed me his story which appeared after the murder in *The Sunday Times*. Headed, "Army sweetheart meets cruel death", the story was based on articles in the Israeli press where allusions to Nadia's affair with an Israeli officer appeared without naming Daniel. "That guy will have to pay for it," Fred said gleefully. "An extraordinary case of having your cake and eating it."

I volunteered to do night shifts and worked as many hours as the agency allowed me. Filling the time between sleeplessness and wakeful grief. Nadia became much more than a murdered Palestinian collaborator. Much more than Daniel's other woman. Much more than a woman I had interviewed. Her death was another omen, another strangling hand round my neck.

I ached to see Daniel. To try and make sense of this death. And of his behaviour. I raged against him, but I longed to put my head on his broad shoulders and weep.

There was no place for me to grieve. Rachel's anger did not leave room for my sadness. Colleagues at the agency were hard-nosed news reporters, who had seen it all, been everywhere, covered wars and trouble zones without shedding a tear. Nava and her friends – not unlike Rachel – were politically indignant about the murder but could not appreciate my confusion.

The only person I felt I could speak to about the sadness was Tova. When I telephoned to ask if I could come to see her, Tova was not surprised. She welcomed me warmly. She sat me down in front of her dark dining-table, laden with food, which I tried to force down as I struggled with my emotions.

Death, I told Tova, was taking such a permanent hold, that I couldn't find peace.

"Some people need the constant presence of death in their lives." Tova's very light blue eyes shone strangely in her small, sharp face. "I'm sure your parents knew that."

"Is that why these things are happening to me now? All this death and devastation?"

"Perhaps. It may be possible you have chosen to come here and witness the agony at first hand because death had always been an unconscious, intimate part of your being."

"If this why Daniel works where he does?"

"I'm sure it is," Tova smiled sadly. "Some children of survivors must continually relive the horrors of their dreams. Dani turns those nightmares into reality."

I felt unable to expose my involvement with Daniel to his mother. And Nadia's death was part of this involvement. But Tova knew exactly why I was there, even without knowing the details. As foods kept appearing on the embroidered tablecloth, she ministered to my wounds gently.

When Daniel entered his mother's living-room without knocking, neither he nor Tova offered an explanation for his arrival. He looked tired, almost vulnerable. He sat beside me and said flatly, while Tova was looking at us vaguely, that he had come to take me home.

Neither of us said anything as he drove me to the flat. He held me tight as we sat on the bed, making no attempt to make love or even kiss me.

I turned to look at his profile. His mouth turned downwards, his eyes heavy, he didn't seem the Daniel I thought I knew.

"I owe you an explanation, but there's nothing I can say," Daniel started.

"Nothing apart from acknowledging that her death was of your doing." I felt my anger rise.

"That's how it is," Daniel assumed his more usual, confident tone. "We gain some, we lose some."

"Is that all you can say?" I screamed. "Here in this flat, of all places? You brought her here and everyone knew this was where you interrogated suspects. There are bloodstains on

154

the damn wall, for God's sake. Couldn't you see you were putting her in danger?"

"She knew it was dangerous. She was an adult. A calculating adult. The risks were explained to her very carefully when she joined the network."

"Were the risks of screwing you also carefully explained?" I shouted.

"That had nothing to do with it," Daniel said evenly. "These things happen between women and men."

"Bullshit, Dani. You knew what you were doing. You are always in full control. You chose to exploit her."

"It takes two to tango. I've never made any woman sleep with me against her will."

"Strange tango when one side is under occupation, lost and alienated from her own people and the other is a member of the occupying force's elite secret service."

"Nadia knew what she was doing," Daniel repeated softly. "It doesn't make her death less difficult to take. Nor does it lessen our determination to get her killers."

"Haven't you done enough damage? Haven't you destroyed enough lives?" I was raving now. "First Rachel, then God knows how many others, and now poor Nadia."

"But what's it to you, Patricia? Why so angry?"

I broke down, writhing on the unmade bed behind Daniel's back.

"Your mother says death is part of my life. Because of my parents," I whispered. "She says that's why I came here. And that this is why you have chosen to work in the death industry."

Daniel nodded slowly. "I've paid too dearly for my obsession with death. Lost too many people," he said slowly, sadness replacing his assured insistence. "Do you think I don't lie awake thinking about Nadia, wondering if we could have prevented her death? I've discussed it with my superiors and they say we acted in accordance with the rules."

"The affair too?"

"The affair is incidental. They knew I wouldn't betray anything."

"But is it regular, having affairs with informers?"

"There are no regulations to cover getting involved. The work is pressured and many of us do get involved. That's the reality. What counts are the results. And we've made great strides through our contact with Nadia."

"Poor Nadia. What I don't understand is how you can live with all this devastation."

"It isn't easy, Patricia," Daniel said. "Nadia's death may offer me a way out, but until then, there's work to be done."

"If your mother is right, I came here looking for this pain," I said. "Why am I punishing myself? Do I really need all this death?"

"You ask too many questions," Daniel said. "Why don't you try and find out some answers?"

"What do you suggest?"

"The Women's Therapy Centre has some English-speaking groups for daughters of survivors," Daniel said very lightly. "I know many women who have been greatly helped there. Including my own mother."

Naomi concluded the session. "We all know that we've come here to work out a preoccupation with the past, with death. This," she turns to me, "is why working in a group with like-minded people can be helpful. This journey is long and arduous but you don't have to make it alone, Patricia."

CHAPTER SEVEN

Five months isn't a long time, they say here. In the life of a journalist it is. Very long. You're as good as yesterday's headline. As if nothing you have ever done before matters.

For a woman who makes a living out of asking awkward questions, I'm not very good at asking the questions that need to be asked.

Yes, I did spend a childhood accepting what they wished to present. Never asked a question until that day with Mother, after Alison's death.

I must go deeper. This has all been said before. But how do I get there? How do I find out what it was really like? Peeling the layers. Naomi's clichés make me angry. They aren't much different from my own. The ones I made my reputation with.

Peel another layer. Stay with the pain. The pain which has become unbearable. Particularly since Nadia.

Start with Alison's death. Again. Something cracked when that child killed herself. When was the first time I remember feeling like that? I don't know, Naomi. But you're right. I did feel like this once in the past.

Say the first thought that comes to my mind? Not censor it? The first thought is Father. Yes. Father and what else? Father and me, I suppose.

Leave me alone, Naomi. I don't know where all this is leading. I don't want to talk about it. Look around at the group? They're all listening? Damn it, Naomi, I don't want them all to listen. I don't want you to listen, either. I'm screaming and saying I don't want to talk about it, can't you understand? But you're pushing me. Stay with it, stay with the pain. You don't have to say anything, but don't let that pain go.

Come back to my first thought? Father and me? I'm small, my head barely reaching his knees as he sits. Why am I so scared of finding out? My memories are not Alison's memories. It would be simple to discover sexual abuse. We can deal with it. But my memories are far more complex. Less tangible. I think they have to do with guilt. They all talk about the guilt of the survivors. Tova. Even Daniel in his own way. Not that he says much.

I wonder what he felt when Nadia died. Was murdered. Be precise. She was murdered because Daniel had decided to use her to gain information. This is the crude truth. I digress. But it's important. Daniel had used Nadia. Used her to gain information to strengthen Israel's secret service which works to ensure the security of the state, he says. But I too have used Nadia, at Daniel's suggestion. As copy. Alison too.

Alison dies. Nadia dies. No wonder I feel guilty.

They didn't die because of me, I know. They would have died anyway. A sobering thought. Damn you, Naomi. I know the guilt is seated deeper. I know it started with Father. But what did he do to make me so guilty? As far as I can remember, they never talked about there.

But they must have. I always knew they came from Germany. Knew they had been in the camp ever since I remember myself.

158

Get back to the picture of Father and me? I am small, barely reaching his knees as he sits on the red armchair in the living-room. Smoking his cigar after Friday night dinner. The only time he smoked a cigar. There were no candles, no blessing on the wine. Not like at Marianne's. How I loved Friday nights at Marianne's. Her father made kiddush. I learnt what it was called the first time I stayed with them. And then he tore little pieces of plaited white bread and gave us each a piece. And then they kissed each other. And all the while, long white candles were lighting in a silver candlestick. Perhaps Father's cigars were his candles. His Friday night candles.

The first time I stayed with them was when Mother and Father went on holiday to Italy. I was nine, I think. When they returned I asked Father if we too could light candles on Friday night. He smiled sadly and said, this isn't for us, Patricia. Our candles are already burnt.

I can see it now. I didn't understand then about crematoria and burnt bodies. About the nightmares they must have suffered. But he said it so resolutely, so finally, I never asked again.

I loved Marianne's house on Friday nights but Father didn't allow me to spend Friday nights there unless they were away. You stay where you are, my girl, he used to say. This is your home. No need to go to strangers when you have us.

Of course I understand it now. Hanna was given to strangers and they never saw her again. And he was making sure I stayed with them. But I couldn't understand it then. Thought of it as part of his Germanic authoritarianism.

There were other signs. I was too blind to see them but I am beginning to remember. Conversations about Oma and Opa and how they would have loved to have known me. Said

159

blamingly, as if it was my fault they were dead. Everything was said blamingly, come to think of it. Do your homework. It's important that you get good marks. Get a good place at college. Get a good degree. Never leave anything unfinished. Never leave things behind. Never leave anything behind.

Leaving things behind seemed the worst sin in his book. Now the connection is obvious. But even when Mother spoke of Hanna, she didn't linger on having left her behind. She spoke of it almost factually. This is what we did. This is what happened. Don't ask me to explain why. Poor Mother. Did she make the connection between his compulsive possessiveness and having lost Hanna?

And there was never any mention of being Jewish. Of belonging. I am beginning to understand. My guilt was borne out of our isolation.

Father, Mother and I were alone in the world. Stranded in the island of Ireland to which we were grateful for having allowed us to live there. It took them a long time, not many Jews were allowed in. They were lucky. We had no relatives. No grandmothers and grandfathers. No uncles and aunts. No cousins. No distant relations in America. There was no religion. When other people celebrated Christmas, I was told this was not our holiday. But we had nothing else instead. Marianne would tell me about celebrating *Pessach*, or going to synagogue on *Yom Kippur*, fasting and running around with the girls until they felt faint with hunger by the time evening came and they were allowed to eat again. When she was off school on Jewish holidays, I would sit in class and envy her.

Belonging.

Our only celebrations were birthdays when the three of us would have a festive meal, Mother's *Nussenkuche*, and small presents, always small presents, nothing big or vulgar. Friends never came. From time to time Father's colleagues from the hospital came to dinner with their wives, sitting uncomfortably at the edge of their seats, waiting for the evening to end.

Completely alone. Father and I. And Mother in the background. Quiet. Almost subservient. Why didn't you tell me how it was, Mother? How it felt to live in such isolation? She had friends she met for lunch or for bridge, but she never invited them home, or spoke about them. What did they speak about? I don't remember them chatting intimately, whispering to each other, kissing, hugging. I don't remember love.

There were no fights, either. Just Father laying down the law and Mother eternally polite.

When he died, I felt numb. It was a quiet funeral. Only a few of his colleagues, Marianne's family and three or four of Mother's bridge friends.

He was cremated, at his request. Said he wouldn't have a Jewish burial with a rabbi and all that. What irony. Back to the crematorium he was saved from.

Oh, God.

In all our arguments, I never confronted him. We fought about politics, the youth of today, life in general. But I never asked him what it was like. Never gave him an opportunity to unload. Even after his death, when Mother became lighter, freer to laugh, to sleep a little later in the mornings and go to bed earlier at night. When her strict routine, dictated by his timetable, loosened up. Even then I didn't ask her how it felt.

Why did I allow myself to be so blind? Why didn't I see they needed me? Why was I afraid to ask the questions that needed to be asked?

It's funny that I became an investigative journalist, I who was unable to investigate my own life.

I am beginning to ask questions now. At twenty-six. Almost too late.

I felt personally responsible, for the first time, when Alison died. I suppose this came from having always felt secretly responsible. For Father and Mother's voluntary isolation. For their inability to speak. For all their deaths. For Hanna. Who was always there between us, even though I didn't know about her then.

I felt responsible for Alison's death and now for Nadia's. I suppose I exaggerate my responsibility. We are not omnipotent. Haven't got the power to give lives or take lives. I agree, Naomi. But I do have a problem there.

Don would never have bothered to feel responsible for the people we wrote about. Left his sense of guilt behind, together with his priest's robes.

Are you saying I chose him because I needed to punish myself? But I didn't choose him. It just happened.

Hold on a second, Naomi. Are you saying we always choose? Some cultures even believe we choose our parents?

Give me a break, Naomi. I can't take this on board. I can't stand it any longer. Wait a minute. Please, Naomi. This is too much. I tell you I didn't choose them. I can accept that there has been an element of choice with Don. And with Daniel. Well, nobody forced me at gunpoint. But the concept of choosing your parents is the one I find impossible to accept. Did I want to grow up in complete isolation? Did I need to feel continuously guilty? I needed to learn something? What, for God's sake? What?

Tova says that death is part of my life. That I needed to come here, to where death is the reason for life. I can agree

162

with that. But it was they who put death in my life. Even Tova sees it this way.

I can see the path now. Father and Mother and I and our tacit existence in the shadow of death. Guilt as my inner furniture. Buying into their silence without question. But how can you say that I've chosen it? That I needed to learn something from it?

I can see the pattern in choosing a career as a journalist when so many other options were open after university. I needed to learn to ask all the questions I hadn't asked before. Asking difficult questions and shunning soft stories, looking for blood. Always more blood. And then homing in on Alison. And what I believed was going to be an easy story turned out to be the bloodiest of them all.

I can see the pattern in choosing Don as my unattainable lover. The one man of the many I could have gone out with who would never be available to me. And allowing myself to be driven by him.

And then coming here, when I could have got a job in London or an American visa. Landing in the heart of the war. And then Daniel. And Nadia.

Guilt. Choice. All words, Nadia said. What am I but a word merchant? Covering up with words for what I should do. Covering up for the questions I didn't have the courage to ask.

But I'm beginning to ask now. I've asked more questions of Daniel in a couple of months than I asked Don in three years. And yet I've never asked him about his wife. Accepting part-time love as my due as I've always done. Part-time love. Father. Don. Daniel.

Alison dies and I feel personally responsible. Nadia dies

163

and I feel personally responsible. Hanna is lost and I come here to find her. Is this the reason? Was I born to bring Hanna back to Mother? Is this why I chose my particular parents?

Oh, God. And what if I don't find her?

CHAPTER EIGHT

Daniel

When they phoned to say Nadia had been killed, I felt nothing. Not even rage. What a mess. She had been beaten and then raped. Her legs were twisted in rigor mortis and her mouth stuffed with filthy rags. Her face was covered in congealed blood. Her hair shaved.

Even I, having seen so many people beaten, defeated, dead, even I was so sick that I turned aside and vomited and vomited against the cement wall surrounding the waste ground.

Her sister found her behind their parents' home. She called us first. Nadia had given them the number. In case.

She then called their people and lodged an official complaint. They laughed. What do you expect? they said. And put the phone down.

Our boys came round, measuring and taking photographs and the army hassled some youths around the scene and then everything went incredibly quiet. For a few moments I was left alone with her to wait for the ambulance. The air was still and heavy and only one solitary fly buzzed obstinately above the body.

It hadn't been easy. It took a long time to get her to enjoy making love. When she relaxed, she was a tigress. All heat and light. I looked at her face, ugly now, and felt a lump. I don't know how to cry. But when the ambulance arrived, I averted my face. Before I went home, I drove to the other apartment. It was as orderly as we had left it. They hadn't come snooping yet. I took her address book from the locked desk drawer. I took her desk diary where she marked our meetings as manicurist appointments. She had to keep a record, she said, in case I reneged. I brought some of her things home and locked them in my filing cabinet. My wife would never look. But if they came searching, they'd find them anyway.

I crept stealthily into bed around five in the morning. I knew from her breathing that she was not asleep. I slipped under the blanket as quietly as I could, but she turned over and said, her voice clear and fresh, "Difficult night?"

I mumbled something, affecting tiredness. She rolled over and after a short while started to breathe regularly. Where does she get this amazing ability to sleep through it all?

In the morning I told her about Nadia. Said we were supposed to have had an affair, since I was sure it would appear in the papers. Their people would see to it. She said lightly, "You wouldn't have had an affair with one of them, would you?" I didn't know whether she was mocking me.

I was worried about Patricia. After the death of that girl in Dublin, another death could frighten her. I saw to it that Rachel received information about Nadia and me. To give Patricia an opportunity to discuss Nadia's death and off-load her fears before we met.

It takes all my waking time now to fight being obsessed with Nadia's death. I should have prepared for it. She knew it was coming. This time the bastards got me. It wasn't really

Nadia they were after, it was me. But she's the one who is dead.

The boys joke now. They say I would have to find another woman informer. I even had a call from the boss, suggesting as much. But it's becoming harder with every job. To let go and see them only as suppliers of information. And to ensure their safety.

We had a fierce row after she met Patricia. She accused me of deliberately introducing her to another of my women. I knew I was on dangerous ground. I was afraid she would turn on me. So I pacified her, assured her of my deep need for her. I wasn't exactly lying. I'm getting to a point where I have to start being careful. Not tie too many knots.

Patricia, of course, feels guilty because of Nadia's death. The guilt of children of survivors. Although she doesn't know what it is yet.

I too feel guilty. But I have a good reason to feel guilty. Nadia was my creation. I compromised her.

Sometimes I think I am letting the game become too serious. It's beginning to get to me. Perhaps now is the time to get out. My wife says I would get bored without plotting. I know I would get bored without the sense of power. About the only thing that gets me away from that frightened child, lying awake hearing his mother scream. When I say it, she says it's time to let all this go. Send the aggressor and the victim away. Live. Present time.

I know she's right. But then look at her. Living behind her glass walls, never talking about the past. Perhaps this is what she's doing. Living in the present. And it's I who linger in some fixated past, worrying about Mother, and struggling to change the world.

Perhaps the time has come for me to confront the pain.

Nadia's death touched too many old hurts. I must touch my pain to make contact. Otherwise I live on, without tears, numb. From death factory to death factory we walk the shadows and hope for a ray of light.

The rage at Nadia's death, the rage at her killers, this time more so than with all my other losses, helps to release other rages. Rage at Father for enclosing me within the walls of his obsessive cruelty. Rage with Mother for not talking about her pain. For lying there in silence taking the blows at night, and in the morning singing while she made his sandwiches. Rage at being made their torchbearer, and pity for their unbearable loss.

Losing a child, Mother always says, is the worst thing a parent can experience. Losing a child and being powerless to save her, yet saving your own life, is impossible to live with. She says and she doesn't cry. But live on she did. And I'm the result of this miserable life. A poor replacement for her dead Rivka. Not even a photograph remains. A whole life wiped out.

But then my wife too has no photographs of her parents. She had some, but they got lost in transit. In so many transits.

Damn. We, the generation of forty-five, were supposed to have been born free.

I've had it, Mother. Had your nightmares. Had your holier-than-thou babblings about peace in our time. Being a survivor doesn't make you an expert. Doesn't make you morally superior. There's no peace for the evil. You have given us a terrible burden, but we've got to get up in the morning and sing before breakfast. Toughen up and round up the usual suspects, as we smile with our incredibly blue eyes and flex our emotional muscles, drowning the fear.

This is me, Mother, I want to scream now that Nadia too is dead. Me, who is carrying out the evil work. Me, who

168

perpetuates your memories. But I dare not. Her pain is too brittle, her coping too fragile.

I don't know how she knows, but she's right when she says none of us children of survivors have allowed ourselves to become really angry with our parents for burdening us with their pain. We don't dare. We are bound to their past and the only way of not perpetuating it is by not having children of our own.

I would have liked to have had children. Truly free children with a real childhood, with clean memories to grow up with. But she, who says she'd had no childhood, wouldn't hear of it. And so we live on, she wearing that incredible blond smile, and I behind my brick fences, soldiering on, soldiering on.

Patricia doesn't yet recognise her rage. Instead, she is angry with me. For killing Nadia, she says. Like all journalists, she can't see beyond the facts. Hasn't quite figured out the complexity of our existence. She shouts her incomprehension of her parents, but she doesn't dare shake them off.

As if I could shake mine off. Mother tried to remove me by sending me to the kibbutz. But it was too late. Their pain had been imprinted on my brain by then. Their pain made me what I am. The need for power. The ability to inflict pain. My real motivation, let's face it. Not state security.

Nadia's death keeps me awake most nights now. Her death was the worst. More so than the contacts in Madrid. Or that woman in Germany. Or Micha after seventy-three.

If I wanted to be pompous, I could say we are the unsung heroes of the wars of the Jews. Our names don't appear framed in black in the newspapers when we die. Our funerals are private, almost secret. So when someone like Micha dies, no one knows of his heroism. Yet a death like Nadia's get splashed all over the papers. They saw to it. We could have censored it, but it would have made matters worse. So I remain with a grief I can share with no one. Certainly not Nadia's family. They could even be relieved. She was an embarrassment. And a danger.

Yes, they have assured me in the Service that the operation was impeccably carried out. But between the lines I can hear their doubts. Behind the jokes about running a women's network. Behind their avoidance. Behind their hints at my sexual prowess. There are rumours of reshuffles and promotions, but no one looks me straight in the eye.

This could be the time to get out. Before they push me out. No one is going to win this war. I know it despite what I say to Patricia about the lack of choice of the means to achieve our aim.

Since the beginning of time we've fought a war without end. A war we don't want to let go. We scream to drown the fears. We forego life's little pleasures – an unhurried meal, a drive up the mountains, an afternoon on the beach – in case the phone rings to summon us.

I go home each night and look at her sleeping peacefully, wondering how long we have left. I take her in my arms and we make love but in my body our fears, and the pains of former generations, scream.

She says I should relax when I am home. Says I must make peace with myself. My nerve endings and blood vessels conduct the pain deep into her, but she remains untouched. Enveloping me with a placidity too transparent for me not to see the bloodstains on the carpet of her heart.

The stains of having been assigned to life.

The stigma of having been spared.

The distant memory of parents whom she says she cannot recall.

The lost childhood.

CHAPTER NINE

Therapy distanced me from my everyday concerns. Work was becoming less exciting. Being part of the international press pack had become routine now. I was in danger of becoming uninterested, of treating political events, wars, and more importantly, other people's disasters, which I once considered the mainstay of my life, as mere means of making a living, enabling me to stay on in Jerusalem, deciphering. Deciphering was my main preoccupation now. But the more I discovered, the more obscured the picture became. In therapy session after therapy session I dwelt on the guilt, instilled in me by a scrupulous father and a taciturn mother. And yet I knew that this was only part of the story. There was another guilt, that of being responsible. For what, I didn't know.

I didn't have the space to express rage. And I wasn't getting nearer to understanding.

"I can see what brought me here," I said to Rachel one stormy afternoon, when the Jerusalem winds were threatening to tear apart the apartment's closed shutters. "But I cannot see what I'm supposed to find out. I know there's something there. I knew that journalism merely scratches a rough surface, what more is there for me to discover?"

"Aren't you here to find your sister? If she exists?"

171

Rachel was impatient when I began speaking about guilt, always bringing the conversation back to the practical.

I went along with her. "Something tells me that she exists. What I don't know is how to go about finding her. And if I find her, what do I say?"

"You'll know what to say if you find her," Rachel said. "And you'll find her when you're ready to confront her. And your mother."

"Yes. Naomi says that when we're ready, things come our way. She said Alison died when I was ready to confront other issues in my life, like the affair with Don, like finding out about Hanna. But I find it hard to accept Alison had to die simply to allow me to go on what Naomi calls my crusade. On the other hand, I might never have found out about Hanna if Alison hadn't died." I was looking at a distant point beyond Rachel's face. "But I simply can't accept all these people had to die simply to allow me to find myself. Alison. Nadia."

I returned to Tova. Sitting in Tova's darkened living-room, munching chocolate biscuits, I found it hard to ask the question.

When I did ask, it burst out uncontrollably, almost petulantly.

Tova smiled sadly. "How do you live with the moment of letting go? The most impossible question. Many of us refuse to relive the moment of parting from our loved ones. For years I refused to think about the last moment I saw my parents. I can see them now. Mama, in a blue summer dress, navy shoes, her long hair combed severely into braids which surrounded her head like a halo. Papa in a brown suit, wide-brimmed brown hat, his moustache glistening in the sun.

Both walking slowly towards the ghetto square in one of the first selections. They looked reasonably well. I don't know how they managed it. There hadn't been much to eat and sanitation was poor, but Mama got out her good dress and Papa's *Shabbat* suit. Perhaps they really thought they were going to a better place. Mama kept saying soon you and Shmulik and Rivka will be joining us. That particular selection didn't include young able-bodied Jews, you know. Or babies. Only those over fifty. I knew instinctively this was the last time I would see them but I couldn't help thinking they were deserting me. Who will care for me? I kept thinking. I had Shmulik, but I felt all alone. There are no words to describe that feeling. So final. Rivka was in my arms but I kept her face turned away. So that the picture would not last in her mind. I didn't know then how little time she had left for memories."

Tova paused. "You know, there isn't a day I don't think about that final moment. And about that other moment, when they took Rivka away. The powerlessness is the worst. Here I was, a healthy young woman, a mother, and I was totally unable to do anything to save my own child. Or Mama," She sighed. "But I went on living. That's the worst part."

She looked at me. My face was buried in my hands. I couldn't bear to look at her. "Look at me, Patricia," she said almost forcefully. "Don't hide. It's hard enough to talk about there, but it's even harder to think people can't cope with what you are saying."

"I'm sorry," I mumbled. "I came to you to try and understand my own mother."

"The time will come when you'll have to ask her yourself."

"I know," I whispered. "That's what I'm trying to delay, I

suppose. At least you can put words to it. I don't think she can. For years, to live as if all of this hadn't happened. I remember her from when I was a little girl. Always well-dressed, made up, controlled. But I can't remember her ever holding me tight. Her gaze was always distant, as if she was preoccupied with other things, other worlds."

"She probably was," Tova said as if in a dream. "I needed to have another child after the camp. Needed to have Dani. But what I really wanted was another girl. Another Rivka. At least your mother had another girl."

"I remember her talking about my birth," I said. "She said how long it was, how painful. But that all the pain was worth it, that at the end there was a great moment of happiness. When she saw me. I never thought twice about it. Thought it was only a mother talking about the birth of her child late in life. But thinking about it now, the long labour, the hard birth. As if she didn't want me to be born, really. As if she didn't want a replacement for her lost daughter."

"Dani came easily," Tova said distantly. "Slid into the world as if it was the simplest thing to do. In the middle of the devastation, in a field hospital in a DP Camp in Northern Italy. The midwife was an old nun and she didn't smile even once through the labour and the birth. Shmulik was out of the camp for the day and, by the time he came to see me, it was evening and Dani had already been born. 'We'll call him Daniel, after your brother,' he said. 'But you don't know that my brother is dead,' I said. I know, he said. 'I know it inside.' He loved my brother. And he was right. They all died. I wanted to call him Yossel, after Papa, so we gave him Yoseph as a second name. Our link between them and the future. I cannot understand why he never had children. I would have loved a grandchild. To know that the family lives

174

on, even if Dani has changed his name, our name, to a Hebrew name. They all did, had to, in the army. Stripping the old names away. Stripping us naked. Cutting off the line. Now with the name gone and with no grandchildren, our tree is dying. We are the last of the line."

"My father will probably not have anyone to carry his name on, even if I do have children one day, which I doubt," I said.

"Don't say that," Tova said sharply. "You're still young. You mustn't cut the cord."

"The cord is already cut. Anyway, I don't know that they wanted it to continue. If they did, why did they wait so long to have me? Why didn't they tell me? What were they running away from?"

"You are judging again." Tova touched my arm gently. "The pain may have been too enormous for them to endure. To perpetuate a life they felt they were cut off from."

"Sometimes, when I was a teenager, I felt they weren't living, felt they moved from day to day in a dream. Waiting for night to fall."

"Yes, things are clearer at night," Tova whispered. "At night we could cry. And scream. During the day there was work to do. Things to get on with. A house to run. Copybooks to correct. And I felt people were losing patience with our pain. There were more urgent things to do, a state to run, wars to fight, making a better life. The *sabras* didn't want us to burden them with our memories. Said we went like sheep to the slaughter. Said they didn't want to remember the past, as if every waking moment in this country doesn't feed on the past like a leech. So the day was the time to put on a brave face. Pretend we had put it all behind us."

175

Tova's voice, which started with a whisper, was as loud as a shout now. Her face, small and taut, was red and her breathing was shallow, fast.

I moved towards her. "Are you all right, Tova? I'm sorry. I didn't mean to cause you such pain."

"It's not you, child. This thing lives on in me, I can do nothing about it. It comes and goes, in tidal waves, never leaving me, like indigestion."

Tova got up and went towards the kitchen. "We eat now," she called as she walked. I went after her, saying I wasn't hungry.

"You must eat," Tova said sharply. "It is almost time for supper. I have prepared."

I stood at the kitchen door and, as Tova got busy, I caught a glimpse of her well-stocked cupboards, full of tins, paper and plastic bags, jars, sachets.

"Just like mother," I said, remembering mother's preoccupation with food. "Always making jams, baking, cooking, freezing, storing. It was easier for her to give food than to give time."

"It was her way of showing her love, can't you see?" Tova was facing me now, a red pepper in one hand and a small knife in the other.

"I suppose so. She's a very good cook. Although father never stopped complaining."

Tova pointed to the kitchen table. "Sit," she said, spreading a cornflower-blue tablecloth and laying the cutlery.

"Try this," she added as she put an array of salad bowls, breads and cheeses in front of me.

As I ate, slowly masticating the tasty food, Tova hovered around me.

"Aren't you eating?" I couldn't resist asking.

"Soon, soon," Tova said. When she sat down, I was surprised at how much she consumed. She was a small, compactly-built woman but her appetite seemed enormous.

"Mother," I said on the phone later that night. "I went to see that woman camp survivor. A friend's mother. She sat me down to supper and ate like there was no tomorrow. Were you hungry like that afterwards?"

Mother's breath at the other end of the line quickened. "Are you beginning to understand?" she whispered hoarsely.

"I've started going to therapy. With a group of women whose parents are camp survivors."

"And?" Mother rasped.

"And I want you to tell me. Everything." When Mother said nothing, I added, "It's important."

"I was waiting for this call," Mother said.

"So why didn't you talk about it before?"

"I told you. It was impossible. Your father didn't want to speak. Couldn't express his pain. Only his anger. From time to time."

"Anger is a good emotion, Mother. Or so our therapist says."

"I'm sure. Only his anger was usually directed against me. You remember. Complaining about the food. About the dust in the house. About work and the people he worked with. But never angry about what happened there. It was a historical mistake, he used to say. Wouldn't even tell me about what happened to him in the camp. "

"And at night?"

"What do you mean?"

"This woman I met says that at night everything was possible. The fears. The tears. During the days she dressed

177

up and went to work, but at night she could cry. She also says she can never get the picture of her dead baby or her departing parents out of her mind."

"At night there were only dreams. Unconnected, you might say. Me as a little girl. In the village where my parents had a summer house. Picking berries. Fishing. Running barefoot. Happiness. And then a big van running over the lovely red-roofed houses and all is shattered. Something like that."

"But the camp, Mother. What about the camp?" I could hear Mother breathing heavily, strangely. "Are you crying, Mama?" I whispered, realising I hadn't called her Mama since childhood.

"It's all right. I'm all right." She inhaled sharply. "There isn't much to say that you don't already know. From books and documentaries."

"For God's sake, Mother, can't you stop being so correct for once in your life?" I was shaking now. "I need you to tell me. I don't want any more bloody books."

"I'm sorry," Mother said and suddenly there were sobs. Sobs I had never heard from anyone.

"Mama," I shouted into the phone, but she had replaced the receiver.

When I met Abed Touquan, who was on hunger strike with other Palestinian leaders in the Red Cross compound, I asked him about his parents. Something connected me to this elegant man, now in the fifth day of his hunger strike.

"My father was a doctor," he said slowly. "Why are you asking?"

"Trying to connect. I don't exactly know to what."

"When the Israelis took Grandfather's Jerusalem house

178

after forty-eight, my grandparents moved to the West Bank, where they had a sort of a summer cottage," Abed said. "We were privileged. We had somewhere to go to. But Jerusalem will always be home."

"Was it devastating?"

"I wasn't born then, thanks be to God," Abed smiled. "What are you trying to find out?"

"A link with my own parents. They went to the camp and later, after wandering through bombed Europe, they found themselves in Ireland, where they lived disconnected from their past, or from a Jewish present. And now I find myself here and must make my own connections."

"And you think we have something in common?"

"I don't really know. But I must connect somewhere."

Abed smiled. "There is a similarity, I suppose. Our people were refugees, yours and mine. What you must solve for yourself is how, only one generation after your people were annihilated, after your own parents suffered that dreadful degradation, Jews in Israel are doing what they do to my people."

That evening, at the therapy centre, I told the group about my conversation with Mother and about my attempts to make connections.

"It took me years to get my mother to talk," said Dita, a Dutch woman in her late thirties. "But I persisted. For years she wouldn't tell me about the camp or about her parents. I had to learn how to ask because, when she did talk, I know I asked in a different way."

"I left her sobbing on the phone," I said. "Or rather she left me. She hung up on me and when I tried to call back, she had obviously left the phone off the hook. For three days now."

"You'll have to go to her. To talk properly," Alice said. "I had to move into my father's apartment in Florida for three months before he relaxed enough to talk."

"But I can't go back yet. There's so much for me to do here," I almost shouted. "And I have to find Hanna."

"To present her as a gift to your mother, so you can get closer to her?" Naomi asked. "Because if that's what you're planning, you may find she and Hanna will retreat into a world of their own, one which will exclude you."

"Whatever happens, I must find her."

We haven't yet talked about how I proposed to find Hanna so, when Naomi suggested we discussed it now, I was fearful, yet I was also relieved. I had no idea how to go about finding Hanna, but I felt I was getting warmer all the time.

Naomi and the group members described the official channels open to me. *Youth Aliya* lists. Survivors lists. Jewish agency lists. *Yad Vashem*.

"Hanna may be closer than you think," Naomi warned. "Jerusalem is a small place. A lot of people know you are searching for her but no one has come up with information. She may be hiding. She may know you want to meet her. May have changed her name. And she could, of course, be elsewhere or dead."

The thought that Hanna may be elsewhere or that she would not want to meet me had never crossed my mind. She might have a new family now and not want to be reminded of painful family history.

"Perhaps Mother too doesn't want to be reminded?" I said aloud.

"If she didn't need to think out her past, she wouldn't have told you about Hanna," Dita said.

"From our experience with survivors," Naomi said, "we know that at the end of the day, most do want to talk at some stage, although not all are capable of doing it immediately. Many spend months in therapy, in silence. But they come."

"But Mother didn't ask for therapy," I said, suddenly frightened Mother would never open up.

"No, but she gave you some clues," Dita said. "The most painful moment in my life was when my mother talked to me. Up until then I felt I was living in a laboratory, almost. Everything was always spotlessly clean, everything in its place. She watched me like a hawk, but I felt excluded, you know? She met Father after the liberation. He was her first man. She was still a child when she went to the camp. They married in haste and regretted it ever since. He left her for a Dutch woman, not even Jewish, who was a complete contrast to Mother. Plump, noisy, cheerful, messy. Mother had difficulty breast-feeding me, she didn't have enough milk, her breasts were sore. But she expressed every drop she could and spoon-fed me with it. To this day I long to be held by her, to be physically close. The idea of sitting on her knee, sipping drops of her milk from a spoon, not being really connected, makes me very sad. Yet, when she did talk, the glass cage broke. I was suddenly on the right road."

"I remember now," I said suddenly. "Mother said once she wanted to breast feed me, but she didn't have enough milk. But she was living in comfort, she wasn't hungry, or sick. Why didn't she have enough milk?"

"What did she do when she didn't have enough milk?" Naomi asked gently.

"Oh, I think she simply bottle-fed me," I sighed. "She never said much. Always so busy with Father's phone calls, with housework, with cooking. Terribly efficient, my mother is. There's so much I must find out." I looked at the group, by now familiar, and said, "It's all connected, isn't it? Her silences, her endless efficiency, Father's rigidity. Their disconnected life among Irish Catholics and my purposeless life, the wrong relationships, the searching, always feeling out of place, always feeling shame."

No one said a word. I looked around, alarmed. Naomi smiled very gently, and said, "Do you still feel ashamed?"

I didn't know the answer. "I don't know. I still feel different, you know. Here. Although it's the nearest place to home."

And then I suddenly felt angry. Weary of always feeling out of place, weary of Israel's inhospitality.

I said, defiantly, "And of course the politics of this country is also connected with that ghastly past, the fear of another Holocaust on the one hand, and this macho need always to be the strongest on the other. It's all connected, isn't it?"

That night I dreamt I was in a dark room. The only light shone from a small, high window, throwing narrow rays of dusty grey light on to a big black box at the centre.

Someone was saying, "Don't look now. It's Daniel inside that box. They killed him at long last." There was a small shrill scream and several figures, shaven and dressed in striped uniforms, shuffled into the room.

"Erich, Erich," they cried in unison.

Then Tova spoke quietly, "Leave him die quietly. One doesn't disturb the dead. He had enough in one lifetime, now let him go."

The figures shuffled closer to the box and one started to lift the lid. A man in a black uniform raised a sword and cut the figure's hand. "Move back, Jew," he said sharply. And suddenly everyone spoke in staccato German but, out of the clatter, only Mother's sobs rose distinctly.

I couldn't ask Rachel or Daniel to help me search for Hanna. So I asked Dita, who took me through the maze of Israeli bureaucracy. Together we spent several weeks scouring lists, looking up references. But Hanna Goldman or Hanna Magdenburg didn't appear anywhere.

I told the group of my despair. "I know she's alive," I said again and again. "I don't know why. Something tells me."

Group members said I was projecting my need to find Hanna on to a non-existent reality, but I was adamant. "You'll see," I insisted, "I'll find her one day."

Naomi pointed out that finding Hanna might not clear the picture. "You didn't join the group to get help in finding Hanna," she reminded me, "but to clarify issues so that you can move more freely. Remember that finding Hanna may create new problems, not necessarily solve existing ones."

I nodded distractedly.

"Having lived with a secret all your life, you now want to find another secret, but Hanna may not have the key to your parents' silence," Naomi said.

I tried to telephone Mother several times but every time she was either out or she shortened the conversation with some excuse. The rejection I was feeling, I told the group, reminded me of earlier years.

"I never felt fully accepted. Always an irritation, unless I kept quiet and did what was expected. We were such a silent family. We were always well behaved, laconic. Words belonged to Father and these were mostly academic,

183

explaining a work of art or a piece of music, or telling us about his day at work. Mother said very little. I was asked about my day at school or specific questions about my studies. What little social life I had was mostly outside the house. They didn't like my friends very much. Always said, 'Who is she? What do her parents do?' I was forbidden to have boyfriends, who were considered an infringement of my completeness. My completeness, would you believe it? No one was ever good enough for us. I did what I was told. Performed at school, brought home excellent reports, never got myself into trouble.

"After his death, when I was at university, I let loose. Suddenly I felt free to stay out late, drink – something he strongly disapproved of. But I never had a boyfriend. Not until Don. I suppose I was terrified of closeness. Mother didn't object to my excesses. She kept her silence even then. Allowed me to do what I seemed to want. She didn't know that I longed for her to take an interest, to form boundaries. Of course, having an affair with Don was the last thing I should have done, according to Father's moral code. But I went to the other extreme. To prove that I had a will of my own? To prove that I was still alive? And now, when she won't talk to me, although it was she who opened my floodgates, I feel as I've always felt. Rejected. Ashamed. As if my independent existence doesn't matter. As if my need to know makes no difference."

Making Mother talk seemed as important now as finding Hanna. I'd lived without a past, I now longed for a history. Group members suggested I should write to Mother and tell her what I had told them, but I was afraid. "She may never speak to me again," I whispered. "And where would I be then? Nothing. Stranded."

But perhaps Mother was unable to give me what I needed most? I had done well in my profession. I had had destructive, but stormy, love affairs. I had some friends. But I felt all alone.

Outside the group and the searches, I lived almost automatically. I did my work professionally, covering *intifada* incidents, demonstrations, political crises. I worked as many shifts as I could. Free time had become a burden, not a coveted award. I started writing up my interviews in my few free evenings, compiling the book. I rarely accompanied Rachel to coffee houses. Even Rachel was outside my inner circle now.

It took me several weeks to write to Mother. When I did write, I poured out everything. About always having felt rejected. About the loneliness. About the shame. About having lived with the secret. "I don't blame you," I wrote, "but I need you to understand why I am pursuing this with such insistence. Now that you have opened the way, you must allow me in. Please, Mama."

After sending the letter, nights were full of twisted dreams, days were disconnected. I sweated a lot, although the Jerusalem winter hadn't yet ended and the windy air was cold and dry.

Daniel was waiting for me after work. I hadn't seen him for several weeks. I started to shake.

He walked towards me, put his arm around my shoulder. "They told me you were in a bad way," he said.

"Who are they?" I said, taking his arm from my shoulders.

"People you work with. They're worried," Daniel said calmly. "So I came to see how you were."

"If that's why you came to see me, you can go now," I said, suddenly realising how much I needed him.

"I'm sorry," Daniel said. "I thought you didn't want me near you. I missed you very much," he said softly.

"I missed you too. I'm so alone, Daniel."

Daniel led me to the car, this time without resistance. We drove through the darkened Jerusalem streets, saying very little.

"Are you hungry?" he asked. "I've bought some food. Let's eat in the flat. So we can talk."

We ate from a plateful of cheeses and salamis and drank red wine on the double bed in the empty flat. I hadn't realised how hungry I was. Recently my eating patterns had been erratic. I had lost weight, Daniel said. I should take better care of myself.

He surrounded me with attention, asked many questions, touched me gently but without sexual urgency and it was his gentleness which broke me down. My sobs were like Mother's, big, ugly. Between groans, I told him about therapy, about Mother, about feeling rejected.

"Everything is so connected." I sobbed. "Even your handling of the *intifada*. It's all part of what I'm trying to discover. Is it the Holocaust connection?"

Daniel said nothing. He just held me in his arms, listening intently, caressing my trembling body. Then he said, "I think you're beginning to understand. "

"Perhaps. But what good will that do me if my own mother doesn't even want to talk to me? If I can't find Hanna?"

"Perhaps you've come much farther along the road than your mother. It's her inability, not yours. Shoah families often harbour much worse secrets than having given up their daughter so that she could live," Daniel said.

He told me about his parents and his terror as a young

boy when he heard his father beat his mother night after night.

"I used to lie awake for hours. The room was full of demons. I couldn't understand what they were saying, but I wasn't afraid of the demons because in the next room I could hear Father shouting in staccato German, like an SS officer, and Mother crying for her life, and that scared me more. The living are often more scary than the dead. It was probably why I joined the Service. The death factory. I always felt more comfortable with the dead. When Father died, I didn't cry. I'm not the crying type. They never allowed tears at home. Not in the daytime, anyhow."

"Poor Daniel." I stroked his short hair. "And I envied you because you knew so much about what went on."

"That was the price I had to pay for knowing," Daniel said. "*You're* paying a price for not knowing. There are no winners here. We are all losers. We all live in the dark shadows."

I shivered as he made love to me. "Don't leave me again for so long," I whispered as my body rippled again and again.

After that night, Daniel waited for me every night after work. He took me to the same coffee houses where I used to meet Rachel and her friends. And, when my shifts allowed, he took me to the cinema, and showed me Jerusalem on foot. As winter drew to a close, the sun shone pale and white. For a few weeks I felt almost happy. And still Mother hadn't answered.

The group listened to my near-happiness with scepticism. "He's the only one who understands," I insisted, but the group wasn't convinced.

"You're again trying to find refuge, instead of confronting yourself," Alice said.

"What am I supposed to do while I wait? Keep away from the one person who comes from the same place as I do?"

Mother's letter came when I had given up waiting. It was a long letter, written in a tight handwriting, the letters small and slanted, on pages torn out of a school copybook. Holding it, I realised that, apart from a few short postcards, this was the first letter I had ever received from her.

"I don't know what you want me to tell you," the letter began with no date or introduction. " But I'll try. It isn't easy, after so many years of silence. It's not that I've forgotten. You never forget. The number on my arm does not let me forget. I touch it every day, several times. It's always there. You never forget, but remembering is a rehearsed part. You must train your memory. And if you neglect it, it goes rusty. In my head every moment is alive. But your father and I taught ourselves not to give it words. This is by way of explaining why I put down the phone. Why we never told you. Why I have never spoken. Even when your father died. I knew what a lonely child you were and I didn't want to burden you with my past. We couldn't give you a happy childhood, but I was determined not to give you my pain. Getting through the days was all I asked for. Day after day.

"You judge your father harshly. I know he seemed tough but did you ever think what it was that made him the way he was? I am not trying to excuse him. Or me. But only one survivor could understand what another had gone through.

"It took a long time to find each other after the camp. I went

188

into the camp a very young woman, younger than you are now. He was almost ten years older. But, when we eventually found each other, we were old. Our lives behind us. I can still remember the moment we saw each other. The look of disbelief on his face. He looked so different. His eyes hard. I didn't even noticed how thin he was, or how dirty. Only his eyes. He looked at me and probably saw the same. The woman he had known had disappeared. There was no more love. We could never love again. Can you understand?

"It is taking me days to write this letter. I write a little and then I lie in my bedroom, in the dark, touching the number on my forearm. And then I get up, look at what I have written and fight myself as I want to tear it up. It will take many days. But I know it must be said. I wish I could say I am doing it out of love.

"You asked me to tell you about the camp. And I said there was little point. It has all been said before and the words mean nothing. I can try to describe the dirt. The incredible dirt. You have no idea what this did to us, German Jews, so fastidious, so tidy. Having to live in the stench. And every day pinching yourself and saying I am still alive. What would Oma have said if she saw me with my own excrement smeared all over my legs? And yet I knew she would have preferred that to what befell her. The crematorium. Although I was spared having to see her torn away from me. And I didn't have to see Hanna taken away from me either. I don't know what made us give Hanna to the Magdenburgs. How we knew. But if I had had to live with the memory of her being taken away from me, I wouldn't have survived. I couldn't have.

"Those who felt died, Patricia. It was those who didn't cry, who didn't think, who didn't permit themselves to feel, who survived. Feelings meant death and the habit dies hard.

This is why your father and I seemed so unfeeling. Feelings were death, and to live you had to suppress your pain.

"Yet there isn't a day when I don't regret having survived. I didn't want to live after it. But I did. To live, you had to stop feeling. And the habit of feeling never came back. To live on is to always share in the shame. And the guilt.

"This is another day. This letter will take a long time before it reaches you. But I am determined to continue. This is the most difficult thing I have done in my entire life. More than the camp. More, even, than letting Hanna go.

"You are nodding in disbelief. How can writing a letter be more difficult than parting with your parents as they are sent to the gas? I have never cried for them, you understand. I have never cried for Hanna. It all went so fast and, before we knew it, we were in the camp where feeling or crying meant death. Death has remained my constant companion. There isn't a moment when I don't think about death, when I don't feel guilty for staying alive. I am a fossil, a living creature captured in dead rock. So, naturally, when Erich died I didn't cry. By then I had forgotten how.

"I know I must give you a reason for your life. A life created unintentionally. A life you didn't ask for. A life we failed to make significant for you because of our inability to feel.

"You are the only person I love. In the whole world. I try and try but I can't remember the feelings of love I must have had for my parents. Or for Hanna. I am not mentioning your father. Because the moment I saw him, after the camp, love died. Forever. You would probably ask why I didn't leave him. Why he didn't leave me. We were bound to each other. Bound in the rusty chains of enslavement. Eternity. *Ewigkeit.*

190

You remember how he loved that word? Whenever he saw a landscape which moved him, he used the German for eternity. Our unspoken code. We both knew we were bound. This is why we didn't want more children. Children are a product of love, yes? And yet, he was so happy when I became pregnant. Really. The victory of the human spirit, I suppose. And our bond was stronger than love, I now know.

"I could never tell you I loved you. I tried but I couldn't do it. And writing it is almost as hard. If you could only see me now. A seventy-one-year-old woman, trembling because she has written on a piece of school paper that she loves her only surviving daughter. The only surviving member of her family.

"Another day. Did you ask me to tell you how we survived? Your father was a doctor. He was lucky. There were many Jewish doctors in the camps, but he arrived just after another doctor had died and they needed someone. He never told me, but people said he saved quite a few people by hiding them in the infirmary. He never said, but in his sleep he would mumble words I put together to form a picture. For weeks after one of his Irish patients had to have an amputation, he shouted 'No, no, don't take it off' in his sleep. For weeks. What must have gone on in his head. I didn't try to get it out of him. But even had I tried, he said very clearly several times in the early years that he wished to forget. As if we could. Only once I asked him if he too wanted to die. 'What nonsense, Eva,' he said sternly. 'You must never say this again. Live we must. This is all that's left.' And that was all. I lived every day with my imminent death. I even stacked a little pile of sleeping pills. I would look at them longingly, and touch my forearm. But I didn't dare.

"How we survived. I was blond and strong. I worked hard. From time to time my good looks earned me an extra slice of bread. No, I didn't have to do anything for it. I was lucky. The extra bits of bread kept me alive. As I already said, I was young, younger than you are now. But my survival depended on these extra bits of mouldy bread. Can't you see now why we couldn't tolerate your comments about food? Mouldy bread. Would you have eaten it? Yes. You would. You'd have eaten anything to survive. I worked in the munitions factory. Another piece of luck. We walked four kilometres each day to and from work, but we got extra bread and soup twice a week. Some people were meant to survive, I believe. But you had to stop feeling. Stop remembering.

"And you had to have a reason to want to stay alive. I wanted to find my Hanna again. But that was not to be.

"It's night now. Another night alone. When your father died, I knew I would be alone for the rest of my life. I had no desire to share even the smallest bit of myself again. And now that I am forced to remember, how will I live through another night?

"No. I'm not angry with you for asking. Telling you about Hanna was the only way I knew to show you I love you. I had to send you searching because I cannot move from this room. As I write, the shadows are lengthening around me, like black birds of prey. Take us in, they sing me a madrigal in old German. Take us into your heart.

"You say you are looking for Hanna. What happens if you find her? What will you say to each other? And what will I say to her? Sorry I didn't try harder to find you? Sorry I lived away in a foreign land for so long? I don't know why you are so sure you will find her. Your father and I tried all we could.

192

"I am scared, Patricia. I shouldn't be telling you this. But if this is the last thing I will ever say to you, I want you to know that I am scared. And that I love you."

I read the letter twice. I sat down on my bed and stared at the walls closing in on me but no tears came. She'd spoken to me. She spoke to me at last. The words whirled around my head. But no tears came.

I read the letter to the group. My voice didn't waver and my hands didn't shake. When Alice and Dita challenged me, I got angry.

"Don't tell me what I should feel," I screamed.

"Look at your face, Patricia," Alice said loudly. "You are all red. You look so angry."

"I'll be fucking angry if I want to," I shouted. "You never express any anger, do you? I want to shout, I want to be angry. This is my space, isn't it?"

Dita came towards me, tried to hug me but I recoiled.

"Leave me alone," I screamed. "You are so Jewish. So bloody Jewish."

"God, you are frightening," Dita whispered. "Do you have to take out your aggression on us?"

Naomi, who had hitherto said nothing, looked at me and said calmly, "Would you like to tell us what is making you so angry? From the beginning, in this group, you have been the angriest."

I looked at her. "It's you and your euphemisms," I hissed. "Your empty words. I'm angry because I didn't have a childhood. Because nobody loved me. Because I was always alone. I've a perfect right to be angry. You always say anger is a legitimate feeling, don't you? Or is that another of your lies?"

193

Naomi said nothing.

I continued. "First you tell me I chose my parents, because I needed to punish myself. Now you block my anger. You heard her letter. She finds it hard to say that she loves me. Where am I if even my own mother finds it hard to say she loves me?"

"Which is why you have always put yourself in relationships where you are the loser? To prove to yourself you are not really lovable?" Naomi said in her patient voice.

I looked up, meeting her kind look. Suddenly I wanted to crawl to Naomi, envelop myself in her ample body, sink in. And then the tears came. Until I came to this country I hadn't cried. Now I sobbed and the women moved closer, hugging me, encircling me with a warmth I found too stifling.

That night I dreamt I was in a big hall. On the stage Alison was reading Irish poetry. She was beautiful and healthy-looking. At the side of the stage, behind a green baize-covered table, sat several women in striped camp uniform. Nadia was one of them. Father, in a navy lounge suit, stood centre stage. After Alison had finished reciting, he said into a microphone, "Left," and pointed towards the wings. Alison beckoned to Nadia and shouted "Patricia" to where I was sitting in the stalls. And the three of us exited stage right. In the wings, we were suddenly surrounded by people in striped uniforms who fell on each other's necks calling Cousin, Uncle, Auntie, Oma, Opa. We could hear Father's voice barking from the stage, "All families to the left. Left, I said. Didn't you hear what I said?"

I hadn't telephoned Mother since the letter. I needed time. I brought my dream to the group. Naomi said,

"Congratulations, Pat, you're beginning to connect. What do you think your dream meant?"

"Starting to break free. Going my own way at last."

"But what about the cousins and uncles? Who were they?"

"I don't know."

"Can you put faces to them?"

"Some had Mother's face, particularly the one they called Oma."

"Your grandmother? Your mother's mother? Have you ever seen pictures?"

"There are no pictures, but Mother did once say that I was the image of her own mother."

"You are finally beginning to free yourself, and at the same time setting yourself in a family context, regaining the family you never had," Naomi smiled.

I showed Daniel Mother's letter. His face hardened as he read it. He handed the letter back without a word.

"I'm beginning to get there, Daniel, don't you think?" I asked, my voice suddenly small.

"I wish my mother could say she loved me, even in a letter," he said.

"Why are we so hard on ourselves?"

"You and I, the only way for us to survive is to be in control. But they've taken our controls away, and we remain unconnected. I had to search you out, can't you see? We're so alike. We're both investigators, searching other people's motives, yet not recognising our own."

"And yet you control our meetings. You stay in control, but I'm losing mine."

"You're younger and less experienced in hiding. And

you're lucky to have come here now, before your scars crusted over, as mine have."

"So where do we go from now, Daniel?"

"Do you want me to get out of your life?" Daniel asked. "Is that the way forward? You know I can do it."

"I know you can. Don't you ever relax? Do only what you fancy?"

"I'm doing what I fancy now. Being with you. But I know that it's not going to end well."

I was sent to interview a Palestinian painter who was opening an exhibition in an East Jerusalem gallery. As I was looking at large canvasses covered in surrealistic but obvious symbols of oppression, dark army boots smashing glass doves, and fat women in black dresses flying into the sunset with rockets exploding all around them, I felt a hand on my shoulder. I turned and saw Samarra Haled with another woman.

"Patricia, I want you to meet Mary George. She is an American journalist, who is writing a book similar to yours."

Mary was a middle-aged black woman wearing large framed glasses. "Mary is interviewing women artists working in Palestine today, both Palestinian and Jewish," Samarra said. "I thought you might have something in common."

"What do you think of these pictures?" I asked. "I'm not an art expert."

"I think they're very powerful," Mary said.

"You don't think they're a bit obvious?"

"Perhaps, but their power transcends their symbolism," Mary said. "Look at those brushstrokes. Look at the colours. The power lies in the oranges and blacks that , not in contextual references."

196

"I see I can leave you two now." Samarra smiled and moved back into the crowded room.

I found myself being guided by Mary, whose knowledge of Palestinian and Israeli art seemed endless. She had already interviewed several Israeli women artists, she told me, and she was now finishing her tour of Palestinian art. I warmed to this determined woman and told her about my book, about my journey, about Hanna.

"You don't mean Hanna Shemi," Mary said. "A very good painter. Most of her work deals with memory. In abstract form, of course. She came to Israel as a young child, after the Holocaust."

I felt faint. "Hanna Shemi?" I heard myself repeat faintly. And then I knew.

Mary's voice sounded blurred. I needed to sit down.

"You all right?" Mary's voice came to me from a great distance. "You don't look so good."

"I must go now," I mumbled.

I made my way to the door, followed by Mary who held on to my arm. "I can get you to Shemi," I heard her saying. "Nice woman. I'm sure she'd be delighted to meet you."

Outside, the evening sky was becoming velvety blue. I entered the waiting taxi, feeling suddenly very ill. By the time I reached the apartment, my skin was burning. I opened the door and collapsed on to the floor. When I woke up to see Rachel asleep on a chair, the knowledge returned. "I've found her," I said and my voice woke Rachel.

"You all right? God, you gave me such a fright last night," she said. "What happened?"

"I've found her," I repeated. "And you knew all the time."

"What are you talking about?"

"About Daniel's wife."

Rachel started to say something, but I stopped her. "Don't lie. You must have known. Everyone in this bloody city must have known. She's an artist. She bloody specialises in Holocaust pictures."

CHAPTER TEN

Hanna

Last month I started painting my last picture. My story. The story I've never painted before.

A little girl. I've painted her the way a child would draw. Round face, dots for eyes, lines for nose and mouth and two braids hanging diagonally under her large ears. Her mouth is turned down. They used to say that sad is when your mouth turns down, and happy is when it's turned up. She has thin arms and large hands with rounded fingers, a triangle for a torso and thin legs with five short lines for toes.

The girl stands in the centre of the canvas, my largest ever. I've given her yellow hair, sea blue dots for eyes and a red line for mouth. Her dress is white, although something tells me it should be grey.

My last picture.

After I complete it, there will be no more pictures. I've painted too much and none of my pictures has brought me home.

When I had my exhibition last year, one critic wrote about my obsession with Shoah themes. "This painter is stuck," he wrote. "I don't want to be unkind, but there's been no progression in her work since she started exhibiting. I understand her obsession, we all share it. But she's allowed her technique to stagnate, she's repeating herself, she's telling the same story. I, for one, would like to see her attempt something else."

What really annoyed me was that he ignored the *Kindertotenlieder* series. The pictures on the death of children in the *intifada* and in the Shoah which hung side by side. He said I was stuck in the past, but I was working on present materials.

People said he was insensitive. Other critics singled out this exhibition, said I had reached a new degree of sophistication in linking painful past memories to painful present reality.

What nonsense. I have no painful memories. No memories at all. My work is an attempt to make memory come.

Nothing worked. I tried therapy of all kinds. Psychoanalysis. Group therapy with other survivors. Gestalt. I talked a lot, listened to others come out with the most incredible pain. But nothing came. That critic was right in one respect. I had become obsessed with finding my memory and allowed my work to repeat itself. Even with *Kindertotenlieder*. I listened to Mahler while I painted, but even the music didn't bring me there. Songs on the death of children. It should have brought some feelings. But the pictures allowed me to shut myself off.

I envy him at times. At least he knows. However painful it is. And his mother, with her detailed, compulsive recall. And those countless others whose memories are clear, whose every day is full of waking nightmares. Only I am deprived of memories. So I painted on, in the hope that through visual associations – the only ones I have at my disposal, for I'm not a word person – something will come.

Of course I wonder about my parents. But no pictures come. And no feelings. So I hide behind my oil paints and canvas, mix colours and cover canvas after canvas with pathetic attempts to remember.

But something happened in the last few weeks. Since that Palestinian woman was murdered. The one he is supposed to have slept with. He told me about it, because he felt guilty. He knows I don't care about his women. But this time it was different. I've never seen him so distraught. He shouts in his sleep. He spends more nights away from home and creeps into bed before dawn, smelling of other places. As if that woman's blood is on his hands. And he's started to spend time on his thesis again. Preparing to leave the Service?

I don't know what it is, but his pain, never before so apparent, is starting to make pictures in my head. The pictures speak so loud that at times I, too, want to shout. Of course I never shout. I don't think I know how.

I've been thinking about this picture for some weeks now. From the start I could see the little girl, drawn in childish lines, her hair yellow and her eyes blue. But, until I started painting, I couldn't see the rest of the picture.

It's filling up slowly, my last picture. The girl has grown as the days go by. She almost fills the entire canvas now. But there are other things in the picture. A small house in flames. Painted carefully with many details in the upper left-hand corner. And a tiny line of people queuing for bread, drawn almost photographically, with faces borrowed from a photograph I've seen of bombed Berlin. On the girl's white dress there is a rail wagon in strong red, like a child's toy, and through one window there's the blank face of an old woman. And somewhere there's a tiny faded sepia photograph of a mother, a father and a little blond girl, whom I carefully avoided giving faces to.

I haven't finished painting it yet. I told him I was painting my last picture because, at last, memory was starting to form vague images, somewhere in the back of my brain.

He looked at me sadly and said, "It may be closer than you think."

But when I asked him to explain, he shrugged and went back to his desk. He didn't talk to me that whole day, and I sat staring at my canvas, unable to paint. But I came back to it.

I can't say it's painful. I've never felt pain.

At least he knows. He has felt pain. But all I've ever felt is the soft emotions of the numb. He laughs and says he's blessed with a wife who asks no questions, who feels no jealousy. He doesn't say his wife has no feelings. Full stop. And at times I think he'd prefer me to make scenes.

I've always been lucky. To have no parents or childhood memories, yet to find myself here, at the age of six, a pretty blonde, loved by everybody. That must have been the best thing that could have happened to an orphan.

I have a vague memory of a woman who asked me about my parents. She was American, I think. I suppose I couldn't tell her, because I didn't know. I might have told her about Uncle and Auntie Magdenburg and how their house was gone. I told her I thought they weren't my real parents. But I couldn't remember any names. And then there was the big boat, and the transit camp, and then there were Shlomo and Hava.

In the moshava I was the blondest girl and everybody

wanted to be my friend. Shlomo and Hava had four new children and we all lived in a small room, two boys and two girls. Katia, Moshe and David were always in trouble but I didn't seem to share their unrest. Apart from which, the art teacher at our school showed me how to paint. 'You're going to be a famous artist one day,' she used to say, and Shlomo and Hava smiled proudly. Only the bad news of the other three marred the calm. From time to time social workers and police looked for Moshe and David, or came to talk about Katia. Shlomo and Hava would pat me and say I was their good little girl. When I was sixteen, Shlomo and Hava were killed in an accident. I moved to Tel Aviv and worked in a cafe and painted at night in a rented room in Hayarkon Street, overlooking the sea.

I painted sunny landscapes and portraits. My canvases hung on the walls of the army base where I served. Art school changed my style completely. I followed the artistic trends and painted large, colourful, abstract shapes, selling moderately and enjoying a certain reputation.

It was he who introduced the Shoah to my pictures. I met him at an exhibition. He was already in the Service and, as he is fond of reminding me, he strayed into the exhibition in search of a mysterious girl he had met a few days previously, and who told him she had a picture hanging in our exhibition. He never found his girl.

"You are so blond," he said and looked at me with his amazingly blue eyes. "Are you German?"

After that night, when he told me about his parents as we lay on my bed, I could paint no more landscapes or abstracts. For almost twenty years now I've been painting his internal scapes, in a futile attempt to make my own memories.

From time to time I've tried to look for my real parents, whom I cannot remember. The Germans have been very helpful in trying to find the Magdenburgs' papers, but nothing survived from that street. No documents as to who gave me to them.

He says I don't really want to find my past. He may be right. I didn't really try too hard. He says I shut myself up behind a glass wall, allowing life to pass me by.

I married him because he linked me to the present. I had no past, but I lived in limbo, not really in the present. His daily concerns with security, his taciturn toughness, allowed me a window. I married him because his pain was so near the surface. Something in me needed his pain. Perhaps I hoped it would bring me back to my lost memories.

"But why did you marry me?" I often ask him that. He laughs and says he loves my Germanic looks. My placidity.

I think he married me because I seemed so unruffled. Today I'd call it numb. And because I needed his pain. Because he needed me to bear witness to his unending thirst for control, and because he knew I wouldn't stop him as long as he came home. You could say it was love, of a sort. You could say it was despair. Two shipwrecked children, clinging to each other .

Few people can see his pain. He is the arrogant face of Israeli occupation, the controlling, manipulating force, behind the face of the professional soldiers who insist theirs is a survival war. Even his mother is not always sure of his feelings. When we go out with his colleagues, they treat me respectfully. The famous painter, whose husband is sleeping around, must be handled with care. I laugh at their caution and from time to time let drop hints which scandalise these ultra-conservative men and women.

He knows I know. And he knows it makes no difference. My life runs between the garden, where I grow my herbs and my flowers, and the studio, where I wait for him to come home.

I've never wanted children. He no longer does. There's little point now. My pictures are my children, I used to say when he talked about it. Children die, I said to him. Or their parents disappear. Open your eyes to what's happening around you, I used to say, with Mahler in the background.

We make love infrequently. I never was one for love-making. Lovemaking is a strange expression. You can't make it. Love isn't something you do in bed. It's something you feel. And my feelings are slow and infrequent. So he makes his love elsewhere, but he always comes home and climbs into my bed in silence. And from time to time I allow him to hold me. Contain my void.

My last picture is almost done, but I'm afraid to finish it. Memory has not returned, and I know that if I declare it complete, the road back is blocked forever. I'll work on it for a while longer, although I'm not sure what I'm trying to find.

CHAPTER ELEVEN

Daniel

Rachel phoned today. It's rare for her to pick up the phone, but this was an emergency, she said, before I had a chance to say anything. "Pat knows," she whispered. "And I've never seen her so hurt. You must do something."

"What should I do?" I said. Like a little boy asking his mother for advice. Only I could never ask mine.

"I don't know," Rachel said. "She doesn't want to talk to me. Says I knew, and didn't tell her. She's been in her room since last night. Locked herself in, and won't answer me. She hasn't even cried, for God's sake. She's tough, that one. Almost like us."

"Should I come over?" I asked.

Rachel laughed. "Stop asking me questions. You should think hard what to say to Hanna. She too will want some answers."

I said nothing and then she said, slowly, enunciating each word, "You've engineered it all, Shemi, haven't you? You picked up that girl because you knew."

"Hold it," I said. "I picked her up because of another business. We've got interests in Ireland. You know that. You covered the Leila case, didn't you? It was important to

207

monitor anyone who came from Ireland. But she turned out to be a Jew, and a pretty harmless reporter."

"But you knew she was looking for her sister from the start. She said she told you."

"But you knew too," I said. "You knew she was looking for Hanna, and you didn't help her."

"I knew and I didn't know. I knew Hanna came here as a child. And I knew Patricia's sister's name was Hanna. But it didn't have to be the same woman."

"We're in it together, Rachel," I said.

"We've been in it together since the kibbutz," Rachel said.

"Bullshit, Rachel. We're in this together, but nothing else."

"Bullshit you, Shemi. You keep me in your sights forever. At least I know I'm in good hands. What a joke – a radical left-winger like me, watched over by the Service. Making sure the woman you screwed when she was still a little girl comes to no harm. You hassle me from time to time, search my apartment every couple of years, to cover up for the fact that what you're really doing is making sure I'm safe."

"So you know."

"I've always known. Known you'd never let me go. You never let anyone go. Look at your list of victims. Nadia Bushari is only the last of them. I was the first."

"Thank God you're still alive," I said.

But she laughed. "What do you know about being alive? You've been in the death factory for too long."

"You're right. I've been there since I was born," I said.

And she said, "Sorry, I know."

"You know nothing," I said. Angry now. "You know nothing about the long nights of terror when Father and

Mother screamed and cried. You know nothing about the days when she spoke about the camps as if it was her personal odyssey. As if everyone who wasn't there owed her, because she was there. You know nothing about her screaming at me, 'For that I survived Auschwitz?' every time I didn't finish my meal. You know nothing about wanting to be like you, like the children born in this land. To laugh without dreading her scolding. 'There's no laughter for the torchbearers,' she would say whenever I enjoyed a joke. You know nothing of the struggle to overcome the fear, every waking moment. Of the choice of going over to the other side, just to silence those voices. And you know nothing of living beside a woman who remembers nothing, but who paints dead children every single day."

I stopped and I heard Rachel breathing. We said nothing for a while, then she said, "You'd better think about your next move, Shemi. There's a lot at stake here."

"I wish you weren't so angry with me," I said. "You are what I always wanted to be. With your laughter and your freedom. You were from here, and I needed you to contain my otherness."

"And what did you need to contain with Hanna? And with Nadia? And now with Patricia?"

"Different things," I said. "I'm a collector of missing pieces, can't you see?"

"But your missing pieces are real people, real women, who have needs too." Rachel paused and then said, "I'm not angry with you any more, Shemi. For years I thought this was how things had to be. I loved you and I was flattered that you loved me. Or did what looked like love. Recently I realised that in today's terminology it would have been called child abuse. But then time passed, and I know now it was

209

you who were the child. Not I. I pity you now, Shemi. You're facing your most complicated operation yet."

"Thank you," I said. "It will be over soon."

I dialled our number. Hanna's voice was sleepy. "How's the picture going?" I asked.

"I'm working," she laughed softly.

"And has memory come?"

"Not yet, but it's breathing hard," she said and we laughed.

When we stopped laughing, I said there was something I needed to talk to her about. But that I had a few things to do before I came home.

"Something special?" she asked in her sleepy voice.

"Something very special, Hanna. Something which will change our lives. Forever."

"You sound very melodramatic," Hanna said. "What could be so special?"

"I can't discuss it on the phone," I said, "I'll be home as soon as I can."

"Are you leaving the Service?" she asked.

"It's much more special than that," I said.

"All right." She sighed. "I'll see you when I see you."

I wish she nagged. I wish she sounded like she really wanted to know what I had to tell her. But Hanna had always been like this. Would I be able to explain to her, or to Rachel, that I wanted Patricia to find out, for Hanna's sake? Even though I would most probably lose her now?

Would I be able to explain it to Patricia?

I've often had visions of breaking Hanna's blond head open to let her memories flow. But I was never sure she wanted to remember. There are enough of us who remember too much. Why should Hanna's life be destroyed by memory? For years I had wanted to shake her placidity, although it was her placidity which attracted me to her. She was the port to my shipwreck. I was the anchor to her still water. And so we lived. I with Mother's memories. Hanna without a past. I with my quest for power. Hanna with her silence.

And then Patricia came. A godsend. Through her I could now fill Hanna's gaps. I suppose I wanted to see Hanna tortured. I wanted her peaceful sleep to be as restless as mine. I wanted her to share my nightmares.

CHAPTER TWELVE

I've found her, Mama. Your daughter. Your Hanna. She's the wife of a man I'm having an affair with. Another mess. You didn't think I would find her. You weren't sure what I would say to her. You didn't really want me to find her, did you? I haven't met her yet. I must think before I make the next move. The next move is going to be mine. I won't let Daniel pull my strings. Rachel can't be my guide any more. I must stay here until I know what to do next. How to introduce myself to her. What to say.

"Hello. My name is Patricia Goldman. You don't know me, but I'm your sister."

No. That doesn't sound right. "Hello, is this Hanna Shemi? I hear that you came to Israel as an orphan. I happen to know who your parents are."

No. That sounds dreadful. "Hello, I'm an Irish journalist doing a book about Israeli and Palestinian women. Someone suggested I interview you. I believe you came here as an orphan after the war."

But that's deception.

When that American mentioned Hanna Shemi, I felt faint. But the fear has gone. Strange. The fear I felt since Alison has suddenly gone.

It defies logic. I should be afraid. What if Hanna doesn't want to see me? What if she says, nonsense, this isn't my life at all?

But, strangely, I'm not afraid. Even if she doesn't want to see me. Even if I don't know what to say.

CHAPTER THIRTEEN

I didn't want to go. I didn't want to follow Daniel into the car. But, when his voice outside my closed door said she was waiting, I had to. I opened the door and he stood there, his face dark as a rain-cloud and said only "Come to her, Patricia, she knows you're on your way."

He said, "There's someone you need to meet, Hanna. I'll be bringing her here this evening. To your studio. It's important that she sees your last picture."

"Who is she?" I asked, but something in his eyes made me accept his silence. "If you must, bring her," I said.

I wanted to say, "Be careful, Hanna, say you don't want to meet her. It'll hurt." But I didn't, I knew I was going to break her apart. For the first time in my life. Something I'd wanted to do more than anything. I was terrified of what it would do to her. Terrified for myself. A terror like that early childhood stifled scream, hidden deep down.

He rings the bell. How strange, I think, ringing the bell of his own house. There is time to take in a stone house, surrounded by flowers, on the hilly outskirts of the city. The door doesn't open immediately. He rings again. He hasn't

215

spoken since he collected me from Rachel's. I don't ask any questions. I don't say I am angry.

When the door opens after what seems like an eternity, Hanna stands there, tall, serious, her eyes like Mother's. She looks at Daniel and then at me, her gaze straight, asking no questions.

"This is my wife, Hanna," Daniel says to me.

I put out my hand. She squeezes it, her touch dry, warm.

"This is Patricia Goldman," I hear him say, "she's a journalist, from Ireland."

Hanna smiles and asks me in. Her English is lightly Germanic, not unlike Mother's. She leads me into an airy living-room, indicating a red sofa.

"Patricia once had a sister," I hear Daniel's voice and I know he hasn't told her.

"It was the only way I could make you come here," he answers my hurt gaze. "I wanted you to tell her yourself."

Daniel comes in with this young woman. One of his conquests? He never brought them here before. I look at her, and I feel no jealousy. What's wrong with me, I keep thinking. My husband brings me his woman, and I feel nothing. They look well rehearsed, their steps balanced, their bodies moving in unison. It is outside my sphere, this togetherness.

"Patricia here once had a sister," Daniel says. I look at his darkening face without comprehension.

"You never brought me one of your women before," I whisper, surprised at the darkness of my voice. "I told you I don't care about your women," I say, and I see waves of pain crossing the woman's face.

"Hanna," she says, her round eyes staring at me, trying to tear me open, "Hanna."

"What Patricia is trying to tell you," I say, "is that you're her sister."

Hanna looks at me, her beautiful mouth curving in a crooked smile. "I don't need your women here, Dani," she says, her voice just above a whisper. "It doesn't matter to me, do you understand? Do you want to marry her? It doesn't matter to me," she repeats.

"Patricia is your sister," I say again. But Hanna doesn't hear me.

"My parents, Eva and Erich Goldman, once had a daughter," I start. "Her name was Hanna."

Hanna looks at me, her gaze distant. Is she still thinking of me as Daniel's mistress? As if that matters now.

"They gave her away. Before the camp. And they never found her," I say.

Hanna doesn't hear me. "Hanna, listen to me," I start shouting. I get up and put my hands on her shoulders, facing her, and I shake her.

"They gave her to a couple called Magdenburg," I hear her say. "Magdenburg. Don't you remember?"

"Magdenburg," I repeat slowly. "Yes, Magdenburg."

Hanna falls to the floor. I rush to pick her up in my arms. I lay her on the bed. Patricia follows me to the bedroom, her breathing fast, irregular. Hanna's head lies, blond, motionless, on the lavender pillow.

"Hanna, wake up," I say. "Hanna."

I slap her face. She opens one eye, sees me and closes it again.

"Stay with her," I say, "I'll get something."

I put my hands on Hanna's forehead. It's damp and cold.

"Hanna," I whisper, "I found you."

Hanna opens her eyes and looks at me. Her mouth opens but no sounds come.

"Don't speak," I say. "We've got the rest of our lives to say everything we need to say."

Hanna sighs and closes her eyes. Daniel returns and lays a wet towel on her forehead but Hanna, as if she knows he is there, doesn't move. Her breathing is regular. I find it hard to breathe.

I wake up as if from a long sleep. Above me I see Daniel's hand caressing my forehead. Behind him this woman's face. She said Magdenburg, I remember, and something resembling pain pierces my stomach. The woman's face is marked by worry wrinkles, but her eyes are clear. I look at Dani's face and it is almost black, like sometimes in his sleep.

"Try again," I hear his voice, "please try again."

"Hanna," I whisper, "Hanna Goldman." It's clear Hanna doesn't recognise the name. "There's a long story I must tell you, Hanna." I start again, "You recognise the name Magdenburg, yes?"

"She doesn't remember anything before that." I hear Daniel's voice. "Magdenburg is her first memory. You'll have to tell her everything."

Hanna sits up, suddenly. She looks at me with Mother's eyes and says something in German.

"I don't understand," Patricia says, "they didn't teach me any German."

218

I look at Hanna and she's no longer mine. Her eyes are those of a stranger. She looks around the room, as if she's never been here before, never slept here, never made love here, never dreamt here. I feel a great sense of loss. I know that when she begins feeling anger, there will be no room for me in her life.

I feel I should fill the silence. "I found Patricia during a routine job. I told you she's a journalist. She told me she had a sister once, that her parents gave her sister away, to be saved. It took some time to put the pieces together."

"You're not telling her the whole story," I say, my anger blocking my throat like a lump. "That you knew and you waited for me to find out."

Hanna looks from Daniel to me, her eyes clouded. I know I have to reach her, so I look her straight in the eye and say "Let me tell you about your parents."

She blinks and says nothing. Where to start? I tell her about Alison's death. About what Mother told me. About coming to Israel.

She talks and talks and all the while I sit up on my bed and look at the wall. No pictures come. She says my parents (my parents?) gave me to Uncle and Auntie Magdenburg, to be saved. She says it again and again. But she talks about a girl who killed herself and I can't see the connection. It's getting dark and the woman is still talking. She's talking about Daniel now. About how he led her along the dark corridors of his pain.

"I know all about his pain," I whisper. And the woman nods sadly.

"You spoke to me," Patricia whispers. She puts out a hesitant hand and strokes Hanna's hair. "Your eyes are so like Mama's," she whispers, "but Mama is not so blond."

Hanna says again, "I know his pain," and Patricia says, "Yes, I'm sure you do. I'm sure he showed it only to you."

Hanna buries her head in her hands and her voice is muffled when she says, "I am a specialist in his pain, it's my pain that I'm still searching for."

"Patricia has the key," I say softly and, when Hanna looks at me, I see anger. For the first time.

"Who told you I wanted a key?" Hanna says to Daniel, her voice strangled by thin hatred. "Did I ask you for a key? Did I ask you for a sister?"

I shudder. What if all this is a terrible mistake? What if Hanna rejects me, now that I found her? I want to hold her, to hug her, but she is too far away.

Daniel says slowly "It's no longer only what you want, Hanna. There's also Patricia, and your mother, to consider. And me."

I think something softens in Hanna when I say she must consider Patricia, and her mother. Hanna, I realise suddenly, had never considered anyone but herself. Growing up alone, unable to connect, she has never experienced the give and take of relationships. I allowed her to live near me, within her glass cage, making no demands. I allowed her not to have children. I didn't push her to find her parents. And now I'm asking her to consider the feelings of others.

I suddenly feel terribly alone. I've lived beside this woman for almost twenty years and I never got close enough to make real demands on her. Like her, I stayed in my own enclosure. For a long time I wanted to shatter her silence, yet keep my own. And the old fear is beginning to take hold.

Hanna's eyes circle the room, her stare vague. Suddenly she focuses on me.

"Why is your name Patricia?" she asks, "it's not a Jewish name."

A deep tremor passes down my spine. She has seen me, I know, for the first time since I arrived. Suddenly there is no more time. I talk and talk, fast, afraid to let the moment go. I tell her about Father, about growing up in Ireland, about the long silences, the secrets. I want her to know everything I know but the more I talk, the more I realise how little I know.

"I could have been your mother," Hanna says and something resembling pain crosses her brow.

Patricia stops talking and starts shaking. "It's only by chance that I was born," she says. "Mama was menopausal when she discovered she was pregnant. They never wanted another child after you were gone."

"I'm almost fifty," Hanna whispers, "I could have been your mother. But I have no children. No one at all."

"But you have," I say. "You have me now, and Mama." And the tears start coming. "You have me," I cry. "And Mama." My tears fall down my cheeks and I make no attempt to wipe them away. I see Hanna's face looking at me.

"You're crying," she says. "I've never learnt to cry."

"Me too, I have only learnt to cry here. Since I met Daniel."

Patricia cries and Hanna looks on, her expression that of an

221

interested observer. I get up and stand beside the bed. I take Hanna's hand in mine and I take Patricia's hand and put it on Hanna's. With my free hand, I stroke Patricia's wet face and then Hanna's dry face. Hanna sends me a quizzical look but says nothing. The atmosphere is charged and I feel sexually aroused. I have to leave the room. I want to touch them both, to encircle them, to let them enter me, to enter them.

But I do leave the room. I go to the kitchen and put on the kettle.

Daniel returns with a tray of coffee and cakes which he places on my bedside table. Patricia has stopped crying. She is lying across the bed now, her head in my lap. From time to time I touch her head with my hand. Carefully. She feels far away, veiled.

Daniel pours black coffee into the red mugs and taps Patricia on the shoulder. She sits up, startled, but accepts the coffee without a word. I drink and the bitter liquid fills me with familiar warmth. But I'm still numb. We drink in silence. None of us touches the cake.

"Where do we go from here?" Patricia asks.

"You stay here with Hanna, until she understands," I say.

Hanna shoots me another hostile look.

"You need to find out, can't you see?" I say. "You're incomplete. All our years together, you've never let me in, or anyone else. Now that Patricia is here, it's your only chance to find out."

"Who says I want to find out?" Hanna says and then, in Hebrew, "You engineered all that. To break me. Don't think I don't know. You needed to see me on my knees."

"I wanted to break you," I answer in English, "but not

222

because of what you think. I know I'll lose you but I'm doing this for you. I've engineered it all for you. I've won Patricia's trust, I've become her lover, I've put her in touch with her own past. Only for you. Only so that you learn to touch the centre."

I know they are both looking at me, but I stare into my coffee cup.

* * *

When Pat fell asleep on Hanna's bed, Hanna allowed Daniel to lead her into the living-room. She didn't recognise the wild look on his face as he tore their clothes off. He stood before her, naked, his erection threatening. Without a word, he grabbed her by the waist and tightened her white body to his dark one. He penetrated her while still standing, and then pushed her under him on the side of the red sofa and thrust into her, large, throbbing. There was no kissing, no foreplay. Only hunger, raw, urgent. There were no words, no endearments. It was almost rape.

Hanna lay on the carpet, eyes open, head hanging to one side, breathing evenly. Daniel lay on his side, his head supported by his left arm, looking at her. They had said nothing since they left the bedroom.

"I feel I need to say something, to explain," Daniel said. "But I'm not sorry."

"You've never taken me like this," Hanna said, "but you looked like someone doing what he had always wanted to do. Why do you need to hurt me?"

"I don't know," Daniel looked away. "You've always seemed so controlled. It wasn't fair. For me to have felt so much pain and for you to be so peaceful. Until Patricia came,

223

I thought this is what it was always going to be like. That I was doomed to stay beside you and never get to know your pain. And I was putting myself at risk more and more. To feel. To stay close to the raw edge. Now that she's here, I could use her to get close to you. Even if it means losing you."

"Poor Dani," Hanna said slowly. "And you keep telling yourself that you did it for me."

"But I did," Daniel smiled sadly. "How could I have continued to live with you, knowing you had a mother and a sister and not telling you?"

"Who knows what we really need?" Hanna mused. "If I hadn't known all this, I could have died as I have lived, numb. I wouldn't have known what I needed. But now, what do I do?"

They fell asleep on the carpet, covered by their clothes. That is how Patricia found them in the morning.

* * *

I make deliberate noises, to wake them. They look restless, even in their sleep. His large hard body, her rounded stomach and small white breasts. Their regular breathing. Like shipwrecks, after a night storm.

Daniel wakes and sees me. He sits up and pushes Hanna lightly. She opens alarmed eyes and when she sees me, she doesn't smile.

"Hanna," I say, "remember me? Your sister, Patricia?"

There is recognition in her eyes but she says nothing. Daniel starts getting dressed, as if embarrassed by his nakedness. Hanna is not embarrassed. Her skin is goose-pimpled.

224

"I'll get you a robe," Daniel says in English and she nods.

I want to apologise for falling asleep on their bed, but no words come.

We eat breakfast in silence. Then Patricia says, "We have to do something. We have to tell Mother."

Hanna says, "I'm not ready. You have to see my pictures first."

Patricia nods. I have to go to work but I'm afraid to leave them. I call the office and give orders for the day, saying I won't be in. Hanna looks at me quizzically.

"I'm not going to work. I'm not leaving you," I say.

Patricia smiles, "Afraid to relinquish control, Colonel?" she asks.

Hanna laughs sadly. "He never does," she says, "even when he isn't here."

"Only you I could never control," I whisper, "whether I'm with you or away."

I ask Patricia to come into my studio. Daniel follows. I point to the central easel and say "This is my last picture. I'll never paint again. You came just before I finished my last picture. How did you know?" I ask. And then I know the answer.

"Daniel knew when to get you here," I say. "He knew this was my last picture. My memories were just starting to form. And once I regain my memories, there will be no need to paint."

The girl in the picture is Hanna. That much is clear. I can't understand where she gets the courage, to expose herself on canvas like this.

"You won't be showing this to other people," I whisper.

225

"Why not?" Daniel says, "It's her best picture."

"But they'll know everything," I say.

Hanna laughs lightly. "Am I that transparent?"

"I think so," I whisper. "Please don't show this picture to Mother, she won't be able to take it in and stay alive."

The girl in the picture looks at me, her eyes round and blue. She is all alone, surrounded by efforts to remember. "What were you trying to remember?" I ask. And then, "Are all your pictures like that?"

Hanna laughs again. She takes Patricia by the hand.

"Let me show you my dead children. Dani's dead children," she says.

She opens the drawers marked *Kindertotenlieder*. She pulls out one drawing after another, and throws them on the large desk.

"These are Dani's pains," she says, "Dani's children."

I feel stabs with every sheet she throws on the desk. These are dark pictures, almost black, done in coal pencil and oil on paper. Long lines, broad strokes. Dead children everywhere. My dead children.

"But this is not Hanna's pain," I say and Patricia looks at me furtively. "This is my story," I say. "Hanna has only started painting like this since she met me. Before, her pictures were full of colour and light."

"And the little girl?" Patricia asks. "Is she also one of Dani's dead children?"

"In a way," I say. "The little girl is his last victim. The little girl is me."

"We've come to the end of the road," I say and they look at

226

me. "Tomorrow I'm handing in my notice. It'll take a couple of months before I can come out. There's a lot of debriefing to do. But this is the end. I want no more dead children."

"What will you do?" Hanna asks.

"I don't know," I say. "And it doesn't really matter, because I won't have you."

I look at Hanna. Her face betrays nothing. They're in it together, I know. In the pain and in the guilt. Where does it leave me? Did I ever make love to this man, who now seems so remote, enwrapped in Hanna's pale aura? Do I know him? And other questions form slowly. About my former life. About Father. About Alison. About Don.

I repeat their names in my head, but no pictures form. I try to think of Father, but there is only a dull ache in the tip of my head. The words Mother, Mama, leave me equally numb. Where have I gone wrong?

* * *

They left the studio after Hanna tidied her drawings away carefully. The sun filled the living-room and cast long shadows on the floor where Hanna's clothes were still strewn in disarray. Daniel picked them up, folded them and brought them into the bedroom. Hanna looked tired in her white robe, her pale yellow hair falling, uncombed, around her white face.

Pat took her mother's letter out of her purse. Without saying a word she handed it to Hanna. While Hanna read it, Pat sat looking at her with great concentration, as if trying to remember something. Daniel sat on a stool, staring at the floor.

227

When the phone rang, Daniel answered. He looked at Pat and said, "They're looking for you. They phoned Rachel's flat and she gave them this number. It's your office."

"Tell them I'm ill, tell them anything," Pat said. "I need time."

"We all need time," Daniel said softly and said something into the receiver. Hanna had finished reading and sat looking at the small sheets of paper, her hand trembling. "How long have you known?" she asked Daniel.

When he said nothing, she shouted, "How long, damn you? Why do you think you've got the right to make decisions for me? For Patricia? For my mother?"

Daniel started to say something, but Hanna screamed, "Don't lie. I'm sick of your lies. All my life you've lied to me. Your women. Your work. All these lies. But not this time. How long have you known?" Her voice was so thin now it was barely audible. She coughed and spattered. And then she started wailing.

It was a sound Pat had never heard before. No tears, no sobs. Just a shrill wail, piercing the cool room. A pure distillation of pain.

Pat froze. She wanted to take Hanna in her arms, but Daniel's look stopped her. He stepped towards Hanna and, with great force, took her in his arms, closing her in a firm hug.

Hanna continued to wail.

Pat started sobbing with Hanna. Daniel's face, his eyes closed, contorted in pain until he too started sobbing.

Pat stood up and he brought her into their circle.

They stood, and sobbed, and wailed.

* * *

I wake first. We've fallen asleep on the carpet, the sun painting deep stripes along the arched room. Patricia and Hanna breathe deeply, their hands still clasped. I look at them and kiss their foreheads, first the one, then the other. Then I phone Rachel and ask her to pack Patricia's things and bring them here. I place pillows underneath their heads and cover them. I prepare a meal. They'll be hungry when they wake. I call the office. Everything has been accomplished as planned. I ask for an appointment with the boss. For tomorrow.

Daniel places bread and cheese, salad and eggs on my plate. He pours coffee into a cup and says, "Eat. You must eat."

Hanna stares into space as Daniel hands her small, carefully cut pieces of bread spread with butter and cheese. She opens her mouth slowly and swallows with difficulty. The evening falls and the kitchen is dimly lit. Around us there are many shadows. I look on as Daniel feeds Hanna. I'm still an outsider.

"What am I doing here with you two?" I ask and they turn to look at me, slowly, Hanna's eyes empty and Daniel's eyes narrowed. "I don't know where to go from here," I say, but they say nothing.

I know it's up to me to find the answer. "I want to phone Mama," I say, "and tell her."

Hanna nods lightly.

"Are you sure?" Daniel asks gently.

Hanna shrugs.

Patricia dials her mother's number. Our mother's number? As the dial turns, I try to feel fear. Or anticipation. But still nothing comes. She's come unprepared, she hasn't even got a photograph to show me. Mama. I place the sound gingerly in my head. My mother. Patricia is speaking now, in English.

"Mama," she says, "I've found her. Hanna." There is a long pause. "She's a painter. Blonde. And she has your eyes." Then her face darkens. "But why, Mama? Please, Mama. I understand, but just a few words."

Patricia doesn't look at me as she whispers "Tomorrow, then, yes? Tomorrow morning. I love you too, Mama."

Patricia replaces the receiver and she looks at me, not at Hanna. "She can't talk. Not yet," she whispers. "Oh God, what have I done? I'm afraid, Dani. What have I done?"

Hanna is very pale. I don't know what to say to them. Then Hanna starts to talk, fast, nervously, in a mixture of Hebrew, German and English. She speaks of all her available memories, from the days with the Magdenburgs. Patricia listens, her eyes big. When Hanna takes a breath, she takes up the story, filling in. Together they weave a tapestry of patchy memories. Hanna opens up like a withered flower. Restored to life, temporarily, by being placed in water. I've never seen her so animated, so eager to live.

Night falls and we're still talking. Patricia tells me everything she knows. About Mama, about Papa, about her own life. She talks about coming to Israel, about her work, about meeting Dani, and Rachel, and Tova. She talks about sleeping with Dani in the Service's flat, about Nadia and her murder. She talks about being opened up by coming here, about the impossibility of returning to her former life. Like me, painting my last picture in preparation for her coming into my life, so she too, it seems, has written her last article, in preparation for me.

"There's only the question of Mama. We must call her again," I say.

Hanna says "Yes, we must. But I'm scared."

Daniel looks quizzically. "I've never heard you say before you were scared," he says softly.

"Are you surprised?" Hanna says. Her anger dissipated, now that she has told me how Daniel kept her alive all the years by allowing her to move slowly from picture to picture, not to have to answer questions. She doesn't look scared, but I can guess.

I'm also scared. About Mama.

I dial Mama's number again.

But there's no reply.